MEMENTO MORI

A Haunted New Orleans Novel

RAYVN SALVADOR

D1452414

Memento Mori

A Haunted New Orleans Novel
By Rayvn Salvador

Be not afraid since life is a story. Live by the words: memento mori.

This book is for everyone who wishes to be a human being instead of a human doing.
Life is too short. Always remember that the second/minute/hour/day/week/month/year before you should be lived to its fullest—whatever that looks and feels like to you. And when you accept memento mori and understand that you will eventually die, embrace memento vivere and go forth and live!

Carpe diem, people. Seize the day! ;-)

Prologue

Hanlen

Then . . .

The images in front of me blurred, like trying to see a penny at the bottom of a churning pool. My heartbeat pounded in my ears, and that ice-water rush of adrenaline had yet to leave my veins. I swallowed hard, tried to tune back into what the man and woman in front of me were saying, but I couldn't concentrate. I could barely breathe. There had to be some mistake. I had just seen Reagan. Had just hugged her goodbye.

I shook my head and tried to swallow, the edges of my vision getting grayer by the second. Just as I sensed my knees give way, I felt strong arms breaking my fall, and heard a feminine voice saying, "Get her settled on the couch. I'll grab her some water."

Barely aware of what was happening, my mind too much a stew of confusion, grief, and shock, I went willingly, feeling my feet shuffle as someone led me into the living room and to our sectional sofa. I collapsed and then closed my eyes for a moment, trying to take some deep, slow breaths through my nose, letting them out through my mouth. I looked up when I heard movement in front of me.

The police officer squatted down and handed me a glass of clear liquid. "Here, drink. It'll help with the shock."

I grabbed the glass from her and took a small sip. I hadn't realized how thirsty I was until the cool refreshment hit my tongue. I took another larger drink, my hand shaking. I almost dropped the glass, but the woman gently took it from me, setting it on the coffee table in front of us before taking a seat on the easy chair to my right. I closed my eyes again. This couldn't be happening.

"Miss Arbor, I am so sorry to bring you such horrible news at this ungodly hour. Are you going to be all right? Is there someone we can call?"

I looked up when a hand landed on mine, eyes meeting those of the man in front of me. There was

2

emotion there, but not what I expected. Not pity, exactly. Empathy, maybe?

"I . . ." I cleared my throat. "There's no one here. No one close. There's only Reagan. *Was* only Reagan," I corrected myself.

I couldn't stop the tears then. They came in a deluge, my body wracked with sobs. My roommate, my best friend, the sister I had chosen in life, had been murdered. I was well and truly alone in the world.

At least, that's how it felt.

Chapter 1

Hanlen

Now . . .

Ten years. I had been gone for ten years, and yet, driving down Highway 61, it was almost as if no time had passed at all. The Spanish moss and resurrection ferns on the live oaks hung like gauze ghosts at Halloween, both welcoming and creepy. Everything about this terrain and these parishes used to be a comfort to me. All of that ended early one morning on a Saturday when two uniformed police officers showed up on my doorstep to deliver the most crushing news possible. Reagan, my soul mate for all intents and purposes, was gone.

She would never walk through the door of our home with the beignets I loved. She would never break another blender trying to make frozen café au lait. Some sadistic bastard had somehow lured her out of the bar where I'd left her, a place we'd been to countless times before, only to leave her bleeding out in the urine-scented asphalt of the alley next door.

The case was still open. Now cold. Numerous persons of interest had been questioned, but there was never enough evidence to hold anybody for long. And definitely not enough to prosecute. It was one of the reasons I'd basically started my life over after I moved to Texas, going into criminal justice. Unfortunately, even with my degree, my emotional issues never let me fulfill my dream of hunting down and bringing Reagan's murderer to justice.

I had eventually accepted reality and left the police academy. But I did log my hours with a great private investigator, got licensed, and opened my own P.I. firm. Four years of busting cheating spouses, background-checking corporate bigwigs, serving papers, debunking insurance fraud, and handling the occasional Amber Alert alongside the cops made for some boring stakeouts and probably the start of liver failure, but I had to admit, I loved my job. I adored making my clients happy and showing the assholes what's what. And I still held out hope that I might catch a break on Reagan's case someday. Because I couldn't let it go. It would likely haunt me forever and be a constant drive until I had answers. And once I did, I would gleefully take away the power her killer held over me and so many others. The asshole would no longer be anonymous. That advantage would be stripped, and they would finally be brought to justice.

My phone rang through the Uconnect system on my Cherokee and snapped me out of my thoughts. I turned down the radio and glanced at the readout. *Mom.* Of course, it was my mother. I tapped the screen to answer and then refocused on the road.

"Hey, Mom. What's up?"

My mother had moved to south Florida years before I left New Orleans, and she had only been back a couple of times since, but she still loved the city.

"Hey, baby. Just checking to see where you are. Did you make it across the state line yet?" I could hear her tossing ice cubes into a glass on the other end of the line. Ugh, I could use a glass of something myself, too bad I was still driving. I crossed some lines occasionally—okay, quite a few—but drinking and driving was not one of them.

"Yep. In Louisiana. Not far out. I still can't believe you're making me do this."

The sound of liquid hitting the cubes came through, and my mouth watered. I could not wait to hit the hotel and raid the mini bar.

"Oh, honey. It'll be great. They just need you to be there as owner of the property. Answer some questions. Show them the lay of the land. There's money in this for all of us since the network offered payment. Some notoriety. And all we have to do is give them access to the house and the outbuildings for the next week or so, and let them film for seventy-two hours. You know your great-great-great-granddaddy would be proud that we're keeping the family stories alive."

I cringed. Family stories, my ass. The truth of the matter was, the Arbor family had landed in Louisiana centuries ago, settling and running a prosperous plantation. Things had gone really well—or so later generations had been told and believed—until a string of bad luck befell the family, resulting in numerous accidental deaths, a few deaths by suicide, and business ruin that spanned the next several decades.

Legend had it the family had been cursed in retribution for something my many-times-removed ancestor had done. I didn't personally believe any of it. It was all nonsense. Bad luck was a thing. So were terrible business practices and people ignoring safety precautions. End of story. At least, they were able to keep the property.

Now, however, most of my family and almost anyone who'd ever stayed at the plantation house—we listed it on a rental site—were convinced it was haunted. Yet more baloney that I didn't believe. When you died, you died. Goodnight, Mary. There was no hanging around—for vengeance or otherwise. If ghosts existed, Reagan would have come to me. She would have told me who killed her. She would have . . . No, ghosts were not a thing.

"—call him when you get there."

Mom's voice pulled me from my irritated mental ramblings, and I realized that I had missed a huge piece of what she'd just said.

"Sorry, Mom. I think we had a bad connection. What'd you say?"

She gave me a long-suffering sigh as she took a drink of whatever she had poured herself earlier. "I said, you need to call Deveraux Glapion when you get settled. He's expecting your call. I texted you his number earlier."

I pushed a hand through my long brunette waves, realizing that I should have had it cut and colored when I was still in Texas, especially if I might end up on TV. I didn't know any stylists here. "Who the hell is Deveraux Glapion?"

Mom sighed again. "The host of *Haunted New Orleans*, silly. I've told you like a thousand times. Did you even watch the show clips I sent you?"

I could only shake my head, knowing she couldn't see me—which was probably a good thing; I didn't school my features well. Of course, I hadn't watched. This was a bunch of bullshit, and I had way better things to do than waste my time watching some idiots traipsing around supposedly haunted locales, playing it up for the cameras and gullible viewers—like my mother.

"Sorry, Mom. I didn't have time. Work's been crazy." I rolled my eyes, once again thankful that this wasn't a video call.

"It's fine, dear. You don't need to have watched the show to appreciate what you're doing. How fun will it be to see the old homestead on TV?"

"Real fun, Mom. It's a good thing we've been paying someone to keep the place up, huh?" The people *I* had been paying, even though I hadn't set foot in the house for over ten years. But I was the current owner of the property, and we did make good money from the rental site—people went out of their way to rent it because of the chatter regarding the hauntings—so I shouldn't complain too much. I could still bitch, though.

I saw my exit up ahead and signaled to merge into the turn lane, a wave of nostalgia rising, threatening to drown me in memories. "Say, I should go. I'm not super familiar with where this hotel is. I'll text you later—"

"Don't forget to call Dev," she said, cutting me off. "He's expecting your call before six. It's important that you guys meet before they start setting up for the shoot."

God, pushy much? "Got it." I bit my lip to keep from saying something super snarky. "Chat later. Love you."

"Bye, baby. Love you, too. Be good. Give N'awlins my best," she drawled, a smile in her voice.

"Will do. Talk soon." I pressed the dash screen to disconnect from the call and turned on the road that would take me to my hotel and the next two weeks of my life. I wasn't sure how I would handle being back here, but with enough alcohol and some progress on this case I had taken before I left Texas and needed to try and wrap up before I headed home, I just might survive.

Chapter 2

Hanlen

Of course.

Of course, my mother or the show or whoever had booked the hotel would put me up in a place without mini bar access or a restaurant on site. It was like they knew. And I would certainly need some liquid courage and fortification for this trip, given all of the hullaballoo I would likely be dealing with. I didn't believe in any of this shit, but the rest of my family did, and my mother was right in one thing . . . this was our family's legacy, and I was a part of that, like it or not.

After some Google searching, I discovered that all hope was not lost. There was a liquor store two blocks down, and my suite did have a mini fridge. Huzzah.

Once unpacked and settled, I threw my hair into a ponytail, grabbed my purse, and headed out for a little stroll. It was only three p.m., and the day was beautiful. I generally preferred fall in New Orleans, but spring had its own kind of magic.

I realized as I cleared the front entrance of the hotel that I hadn't called the host of *Haunted New Orleans* yet. Mom had said that I needed to call before six, and I figured now was as good a time as any. Finding the text she'd said she sent, I tapped on the number and then pushed through to call.

It rang a few times before a smooth baritone came over the line. "Glapion here."

I cleared my throat and tried to figure out what I was supposed to say. "Um, yes. Mr. Glapion, this is Hanlen Arbor. My mother, Linette, told me to call you. She, um, gave me your number. Said you needed to speak with me regarding the show at Arborwood." *Arborwood*. I mentally snorted. The name my family had christened the plantation with ages ago. Redundant if you asked me.

I heard wind through the phone. "Ah, yes, Ms. Arbor. Thank you so much for calling. And thank you for allowing us access to your beautiful home."

Something about his voice did things to my insides. Crazy things. Things I didn't understand. I had never, in my thirty-two years of life, experienced anything like it, and especially not from a *voice*. I shook my head to clear it. "That was all my mother, but I'm happy to help." I wasn't, but I figured I could be nice and at least say so. "I had some business in the area anyway. What do you need from me, Mr. Glapion?"

I heard sounds of the outdoors over the line once more before he spoke again. "Please, call me Deveraux. Even better, Dev. And excuse the noise, I'm running an errand. I would love to sit down and chat with you before the team moves in to set things up at the plantation. Get some history, talk with you about what we're planning to do, etcetera. Are you free tonight or tomorrow?"

The thought of going anywhere tonight or tomorrow made me itchy. Despite being a P.I. and having to be out and about a lot, I was more the homebody type. And, truth be told, I preferred my company to that of others. I wasn't a bitch or totally antisocial, I just had my quirks—I mean, I liked whiskey and maybe three people. I laughed internally at that. But it was kind of true.

I tolerated people well, but I didn't go out of my way to engage with them, and it had been a long time since I'd met anyone who made me want to try. Plus, I had been on the road for most of the day and wanted nothing more than a hot bath and a generous pour after a nice Creole meal. But I had agreed to this. Maybe I could at least push it out as much as possible.

"Tonight might be tough. I literally just got into town. I have some things to take care of later today and early tomorrow, but I could make something work. What time were you thinking?"

I had been walking with my head down and looked up to find that I had missed my turn. I turned in a slow circle, taking in my surroundings, then put the phone on speaker so I could check my navigation app. When I saw where I had gone wrong, I backtracked a bit and turned, only to run right into someone. I dropped my phone in the melee and stiffened a bit when large hands grabbed my elbows to steady me.

I looked up into a face made for sin. Skin a couple of shades darker than mine with eyes the astounding shade of ocean water—had to be contacts—and a full head of dark, silky curls. The man had wireless earbuds in, the same color as the button-down shirt he wore, a brilliant white to match the crooked smile he now flashed me. He held up a finger to tell me to wait a minute, and said, "I'm sorry, I literally just ran into someone, give me a minute."

A declaration I heard in stereo surround sound, coming not only from his sensuous lips, but also from my phone on the sidewalk in front of us.

Chapter 3

Dev

Shock rippled through me. I gently squeezed the woman's surprisingly well-muscled arm and then squatted down to pick up the phone, handing it to her with a half-shrug. "Seems we're meeting sooner than anticipated. Ms. Arbor, I presume?"

As she accepted the device and tapped the red circle to end the call, she shook her head in an only-me fashion and grinned, an expression that felt as if the sun had finally come out on a particularly stormy day—in part because I knew she didn't smile all that often. My skin tingled with that indisputable knowledge. First impressions were interesting for someone like me, a Houngan—a Vodou priest of reasonable power—a descendant of a line of incredibly powerful practitioners of both Haitian Vodou and New Orleans Voodoo. I knew more than most, and sometimes way more than I wanted to.

"And you must be Dev. Call me Hanlen, everybody does, even my clients, unless they're calling me things not fit for pleasant company." She laughed a bit and then straightened her light jacket before running her hands down her jeans. A nervous gesture. Sure, we'd hit reasonably hard, but nothing too terrible. The only casualty in the whole mess was her phone, which I noticed now had a tiny crack in the upper right corner. Honestly, I couldn't bring myself to regret the collision.

The woman was stunning. Her long, dark hair was pulled back from her face in a tail, accentuating the sharpness of her cheekbones and her full lips set in skin the color of beige silk. She had a narrow face with eyes the color of molten amber. Beneath the layers of her clothing, I'd felt her strength in the bare few moments I'd held her to steady her, and I wondered what the rest of her looked like. I mentally shook my head.

"Are you okay?" I asked, looking for any sign that she wasn't, both what the average person could see and what they couldn't.

She tucked a stray piece of hair that had escaped her ponytail behind her ear and licked her lips. I couldn't help but zero in on the movement, and being well, a *guy*, I couldn't stop the images my mind conjured in response. *Merde*, what was wrong with me? I noticed a slight shiver in her body and barely stopped myself from cocking a brow. Interesting.

She still hadn't answered me, so I asked again, "Hanlen, are you all right? Did I hurt you?"

She started shaking her head before I had even finished the sentence. "No, no. I'm fine. Sorry. It's been a long day, even though it's barely late afternoon. And I haven't eaten yet today. Maybe my blood sugar's low or something."

I didn't think low blood sugar was the problem at all. I tried not to pay attention to the apparition that passed behind her. Hanlen Arbor was obviously a natural sensitive if nothing else, though I didn't think she actually knew that. Most quote-unquote *normal* people didn't. They chalked up those strange feelings and times of spot-on intuition as nothing more than coincidence. I, however, knew better—boy, did I ever.

I watched as she tucked her phone into her purse and looked around before focusing once again on me. "Do you happen to know where Goodies Fine Wine and Spirits is? I was on my way there when I called you."

I pointed down the street. "You almost made it before I took you out." I smiled. "John Goode is actually a friend. I can walk you there if you'd like."

"That's not necessary. I'll be fin—"

"I know you'd likely be fine, but I insist. It's the

least I can do after literally running you over. And speaking of taking you out, if you're up for it, I'd love to buy you dinner. My way of apologizing. Plus, I still need to chat with you about some preliminary things regarding Arborwood and the connected cemetery. And it could help that low blood sugar." I resisted the urge to smirk.

She looked pensive for about half a heartbeat, so I decided to sweeten the pot. "Dooky Chase," I said in a singsong. Dooky Chase's was the absolute best for a good home-cooked Creole meal. Nobody turned down a chance to go. At least, I hoped that would be the case here.

Her eyes widened a fraction and then she said, "You've got yourself a deal, Mr. Glapion. Nobody in their right mind would say no to Edgar Chase's gumbo."

"Damn straight." I motioned to the sidewalk with a flourish, extending my arm out in front of me. "After you."

Chapter 4

Hanlen

Somehow, I had two half-pints of whiskey—one honey, one apple, neither of which I had paid for thanks to Dev's good friend John Goode—in a bag under my chair and was now seated at a table with one of the most captivating men I had ever met. Everything about him was simply . . . electric. From his voice to his looks to the compassion and care he fairly exuded from his pores. The problem was, I knew what he did, and I couldn't help the mental scoff—or even worse, a verbal one—every time I thought about it.

Yet, I had to try. Dev and I would be working together in some fashion for the next week, at least. If not longer. I didn't know how much they'd actually need me, but Mom had told me to make sure I was at least somewhat available, which led me to believe that there would be interaction.

"So, I take it you like whiskey," Dev said as he set down the drink menu.

"I do. Probably a little too much," I said, suddenly feeling a bit insecure. *Where did that come from?* I didn't give a shit what other people thought of me. I never had. At least not since Reagan. Why was I feeling embarrassed about my earlier procurement or the fact that I did, indeed, enjoy my whiskey? Who the hell cared?

Dev broke me out of my thoughts. "May I make a drink suggestion? Having lived here, you may have tried it, but depending on when you left our fair city, maybe you haven't."

Intrigued, I cocked an eyebrow and offered Dev a *go-ahead* gesture.

"Sazerac. It's rye, bitters, sugar, and herbsaint." He opened the main menu and set it in front of him, letting me think over the suggestion.

"Herbsaint. Isn't that black licorice?"

"Anise, yes. It's become an absinthe substitute in certain cocktails. But in the Sazerac, it's not overpowering. Besides, anise is good for you. It has some great metaphysical properties."

Here we go . . .

"Metaphysical properties, huh? Do tell, Professor Glapion."

He quirked his lips, clearly holding in a full smile. "All right, for your information, essential oils have all sorts of health and wellbeing benefits, and not just for us New Age folks."

When I thought to interrupt, he beat me to it. "Don't bother denying it, I know you were thinking it. But anyway, they *are* good for a lot of stuff. They're also used magically by those so inclined. Anise is great for bolstering intuition and warding off evil."

A shudder crept up on me suddenly. I couldn't help it. I took a drink of my water to stave off the effects. All I could see were the pictures of Reagan's broken and defiled body on the asphalt. I mentally shook myself to get back to the present. "Warding off evil, you say? And what kind of evil, pray tell, should I be warding myself from?" I swore I heard him mumble something about me being surprised, but I couldn't be sure. He'd grabbed his nearby water glass for a drink.

Just as I thought he might finally address my question, the waitress returned to the table to take our drink and dinner orders. I decided to give the Sazerac a shot, and Dev ordered a bottle of Ghost in the Machine. I cringed at the thought of the double IPA, but to each his own. At least I couldn't fault the man for his food choices. I ordered the gumbo and the cornbread, and he got the jambalaya and biscuits.

And he *was* on brand with his drink of choice. I grinned to myself.

When they were delivered, and I took my first sip of the drink, I was pleasantly surprised. Dev had been right, the herbsaint was subtle and it paired awesomely with the bitters and the rye. Strange, but I dug it.

"Well?" he asked, watching me intently over the neck of his bottle.

"It's good. It's really good, actually. Thanks for the rec."

He flashed me a heart-stopping smile, and my stomach did a little flip. *God, what is wrong with me?* I had never, in all my life, reacted this way to a man. This could be dangerous on so many levels.

He set his bottle down and looked at me intently. "So, what all has your mom told you about the show and the shoot?" Apparently, he wasn't going to backtrack and tell me more about this so-called evil my drink should be warding me from. I barely resisted the urge to shake my head in truth, instead of just mentally. I really hoped this guy wasn't crazy. Well . . . crazier than I already thought him to be. It might be nice to get to know him better while I was in town. Assuming he was single, of course.

I took another sip of my whiskey concoction and thought back to what I knew. "Honestly, not much. She said you guys need access to the plantation, both the house and the outbuildings, and that you would be doing the actual shoot for the show over a seventy-two-hour period."

He nodded along while I spoke, nursing his bottle of IPA. "All of that is true. What do you know about the show?"

Oh boy, here it was. How did I tell him that I knew nothing and thought the premise was bull? *Tact, don't fail me now.* "Here again, not much, truth be told. I know you guys are ghost hunters. I know you're hoping to prove some of the stories my family and others have told about the plantation. Mom sent me some clips from the show, but work has been crazy, and I didn't get a chance to watch them. I apologize." *There, that wasn't so bad.*

The waitress stopped by with our food, and we took a few moments to stuff our faces before he wiped his mouth and chimed back in. "All of that is true, but *Haunted New Orleans* doesn't just set out to prove ghost stories, possessions, and different kinds of hauntings, we also try to debunk them and bring closure to both the living and the dead, however needed."

I nodded and took a sip of my Sazerac.

"I have a team," he continued. "Videographers and sound people, of course. Other paranormal investigators who rotate in occasionally, some who are tech whizzes and others who are sensitives—witches, mediums, psychics, and the like. But I also have an excommunicated priest, two different engineers, a psychologist, and a forensic expert on staff. Their main job is to question everything we've been told before we set out to do a show, and everything we find when we're there."

I couldn't help it; I felt a little better. But I also felt worse. I loved that they had cynics and skeptics like me to balance those . . . what did he call them? Paranormal investigators and sensitives. Seriously? How did one even get those designations? I couldn't hold my tongue. I had to know.

"So, how does one get into this line of work? I mean, what did you say your title was? Paranormal investigator?" God, I was shit at this, the derision practically dripped from my tone. I likely had no chance with this guy when he probably thought that *I* thought he was a fraud.

A rueful grin twisted his gorgeous lips, and I could tell he was trying to keep from laughing. It didn't work. He busted out in a deep belly laugh that took me aback and yet warmed my insides. Strange combination, but there it was.

"What's so funny?" I asked, though I already knew what his answer would most likely be.

"Nothing. Okay, everything. You have a crap poker face, has anyone ever told you that?" He laughed again. "It's clear how you feel about all of this. Why did your mom send you instead of coming herself? She seemed ridiculously excited when we reached out about accessing the estate."

I sighed. Didn't someone somewhere say that

honesty was the best policy? Time to see if they were right.

"Mom and Jake, my stepfather, live in Florida. They have for about twelve years now. They don't leave much. I used to live here." I grabbed my glass, eschewing the Sazerac for my water to dislodge the lump from my throat.

"I'm primary on the estate now since I'm the only heir, and I pay for the monthly upkeep. It just made sense for me to come. Besides, I don't live that far away. A drive from Texas was easy. And I had a case that required me to do some work here anyway." I took a deep breath. "But, no, I don't believe in any of this. It just seems a bit hinky to me. Sorry."

He took a bite of his biscuit and it made me remember my cornbread. I nibbled on a corner as he chewed and swallowed before jumping back in. "Everyone's entitled to their opinion. I'll just have to work harder to show you that what we do can be interesting and valid and sometimes necessary. Meaningful." He swallowed a bite of andouille. "You mentioned your work before. Your mom didn't tell me much about you. What do you do?"

I shoveled in another spoonful of the glorious gumbo and barely held back a moan. It was so good, I had to force myself to tune back into what he'd asked me. When I looked up to answer, I saw him watching me intently. I wiped my mouth quickly. "What, do I have something on my face?"

He smiled and reached out to still my frantic hands as they swiped at my cheeks, my hair, my shirt. "No, not at all. Just . . . watching you eat. I like a woman who enjoys some good Creole cooking." He winked.

And . . . I melted. Until I said, "Then you will love me." *Great, good one, Hanlen.* "I mean, I do, indeed, enjoy my food. And this gumbo is to die for."

He took another swig from his beer and then lifted it in a mock-cheers. "That it is. Though I'd watch that particular turn of phrase in this town." He raised a brow and quirked his lips. "Anyway, you were saying?"

"Ah, yes, the glamorous world of Hanlen Arbor. I'm actually a private investigator. Arbor Investigations. I know, real creative." I rolled my eyes and laughed at myself. "I'm working on a skiptrace case right now. Trying to track down a missing fugitive. Evidence has led me to believe the guy may be hiding out here in New Orleans. I have a couple of leads to follow up on."

"You sound almost self-deprecating about it. It seems awesome to me," he said, before taking another bite of his jambalaya. "And it's a service that people need, and not many can provide. I feel like it takes a certain kind of person to be a P.I."

I snorted. "What kind of person is that? Jaded, alcoholic, antisocial . . .?"

"Wow," he replied. "Now it really *does* sound glamorous. Sign me up! Gotta be better than chasing dead people and delivering bad news that the beloved ghost in the attic is really just bad plumbing."

I knew he was teasing me, and I actually liked it. I tended to turn people off in short order after meeting them, especially in recent years. Dev Glapion seemed a little harder to shake. I enjoyed it. It had been a long time since I could be myself with someone. Maybe even longer since I'd wanted to. And while I was still holding some things in, for some strange reason, I felt like I could let loose with Dev, and he wouldn't run screaming.

We spent the next hour or so eating, drinking, and talking about his work and mine and what would be required of me for the show, and I found myself enjoying the night. It had been a while since I'd been out with someone, especially someone of the opposite sex, and actually relaxed enough to have fun. Dev was great. He may be a whack job who believed in ghosts, but he was awesome. And I could withhold my judgment if it meant being able to laugh like this again while I was in town.

Chapter 5

Dev

We closed down the restaurant, and I realized I couldn't get enough of Hanlen. Sure, she was a bit acerbic and had absolutely no respect for what I did, but I hoped I could change her mind about that. At the very least, the next week or so would be entertaining, and she would provide good company.

Walking out the double doors of the establishment and onto the already—always—bustling streets of Tremé, I took Hanlen's bag of bottles from her with a grin.

"Wow, such a gentleman," she deadpanned and then smirked.

I tipped an imaginary hat. "At your service, m'lady." Which made her laugh, as I'd intended. "So, where are you staying—if that's not privileged information?" I asked, gazing up the way, wondering if she'd walked far from the hotel or maybe had grabbed a rideshare before walking the rest of the way on foot to where I'd run into her.

"Ah, so you guys didn't book it for me. I'll have to give my mom hell for not putting me up somewhere posher. I'm at The Ravisan," she said and glanced at me out of the corner of her eye. I couldn't help but stutter a bit in my steps. The Ravisan was one of the most haunted hotels in New Orleans. If Hanlen was indeed sensitive as I suspected, she was in for an interesting stay.

"So, we have a bit of a walk ahead of us then," I said. "Are you okay with that, or should I app a car like we did earlier to get here?" I smiled at her, gauging her reaction. I'd be fine either way. The night was beautiful, and I wouldn't mind more of her company. But it was about four miles to The Ravisan, even through the park and down Esplanade.

She flashed me a smile, the one I was coming to call *resplendent* in my head, as ostentatious as the word was. The one I wasn't sure she shared with the world all that often. Then she said, "I'd love to walk. It's been a minute since I've been here, and while I wondered how I'd feel about being back, I'm finding that some part of me missed it more than I imagined." She looked away shyly and I couldn't wait to get to the bottom of that trepidation. While my senses picked up that it was something born of the erection of personal walls, I could also feel pain. Soul-deep, personal, life-changing pain. I knew that type of hurt. Had lived it.

We headed off, taking in the breeze and the energy of the city. There really was no place in the world like New Orleans.

"It's so beautiful here," Hanlen said, echoing my thoughts. "I had forgotten just how much, and how captivating the city could be."

"It really is," I agreed. "There's no place like it, and I'm grateful I get to call it home."

Halfway through the park, I felt the energy change. A dark, oppressive, almost choking sensation replaced the lightness of earlier, and I immediately went on alert. Something was about to happen—or already had. Without startling Hanlen, I looked around, searching for the source of the discomfort and any friends or foes to be found.

The faux gas lamps and the moon illuminated the area enough for me to see by with my natural sight, but I still opened myself to see a little deeper and a bit more beyond the veil. A wavering red miasma drifted up from a spot not too far ahead of us, a section somewhat removed and hidden by the nature that tried so hard to reclaim its bounty. I must have been quiet for too long, or perhaps she sensed my tension, because Hanlen touched my arm as we walked.

"Hey, is everything okay?"

How did I answer that? Especially to someone who clearly wasn't ready to have her mind opened quite yet. "Yeah, just have a weird feeling." Not a lie, but definitely not the entire truth. Something bad was about to go down. I just didn't know what yet.

"It's funny that you say that. I was totally lost in my memories and enjoying the night. And then I suddenly felt uneasy. I figured it was just my overtired brain playing tricks on me, but maybe there's a storm coming or something."

There was a storm coming for sure, only it wasn't the type she was talking about. I stopped and turned to her. "Can we go over there for a minute?" I pointed to the spot where evil and despair wavered in the air like heat off asphalt.

Hanlen glanced to where I indicated and shrugged. "Sure. Is there something new over there that I need to see? Something they put in after I left?"

I didn't think what was over there was anything *anybody* needed to see, but I didn't say that. Instead, I instinctively grabbed her hand, not even realizing I was about to do it until it was done. I felt her tense momentarily, but she relaxed almost immediately and actually twined her fingers with mine. An electric shock shot up my arm when our palms touched, and I filed that away for later. There was most definitely more to this woman than met the eye. Then again, maybe it was simple chemistry. Who knew?

When we reached the grove, Hanlen stopped in her tracks, her entire bearing changing. "Dev, something's not right. My investigative brain is screaming at me right now."

"I know what you mean. It's actually why I had to come over here." I looked at her. "Should we go see?"

"Yeah, let's." She dropped my hand, and I felt the loss like a punch to the gut. What in the world was it about Hanlen Arbor that had me nearly tied in knots after only knowing her for a handful of hours? The coming days would be interesting in more ways than one. But first, I needed to get to the bottom of this suffocating wrongness plaguing me right now.

I caught up with her before she reached the edge of the trees, and the sickly-sweet smell of old blood and decay reached me. I knew that Hanlen smelled it, too, because she put a wrist to her nose and stopped in her tracks.

She groaned. "God, what is that? It smells like metal left out in the sun for too long combined with baby powder and sprouted potatoes."

I was sure she knew what it was, she just wasn't willing to acknowledge it quite yet. "Death." It was the only answer I could give. For some reason, I didn't want to lie to Hanlen. She may not understand or accept the world I lived in, but she would grasp facts.

And we were about to be inundated with some gruesome ones.

We walked side by side into the tree line, and Hanlen activated the flashlight app on her cell phone. The LED light lit up the area to reveal absolute horror.

"Sweet Jesus," Hanlen gasped as she took a stumbling step back, brushing into the bag of liquor I held and making it clank and clatter.

A body lay on the ground in front of us, nearly translucent in its twilight-lit death pallor, arms and legs arranged in a macabre tableau. The corpse had something resting on its forehead, right over the third eye. I flipped on my phone as well and took a careful step forward, shining the light on the face. Milky eyes stared up at me, the ghastly gash in the man's throat like a sinister second smile. When I bent over to take a better look at the object on his face, I saw that it was an octagonal coin or token. I couldn't see more in the low light, but I knew immediately that this wasn't good, and had a feeling I knew exactly what it was. Even if it wasn't what I thought, this was definitely ritualistic. It wasn't just some person who'd wandered into the woods and died of a heart attack, or a blissseeker who'd taken a bit too much of their preferred reality escape. This was grisly murder. And sadly familiar. I rubbed my forehead with the hand holding my phone and blew out a breath.

Hanlen suddenly gasped next to me, and I

lowered my hand and turned to her once more. "What is it . . . beyond the obvious?" I asked.

"That's . . ." She hesitated a beat. "That's my mark. The fugitive. That's the guy I hoped to find while here in New Orleans. My skiptrace case." She shook her head. "Well, it seems I found him—though not at all like I or his parole officer hoped."

Chapter 6

Hanlen

My first night in New Orleans, and I spent the last hours of it at the police station, giving my statement and sharing everything I had on Dustin Reynolds with the NOPD. The man had a seedy past, and I'd never invite him to family dinner, but nobody deserved to die like that.

Dev was somewhere in the station as well, giving his statement and account of what'd happened. It seemed most of the force knew him, and I gleaned from the snippets of conversations I overheard that he'd helped them with cases in the past. I wasn't sure what to think about that. On the one hand, as a private investigator, I knew that leads and assistance sometimes came from the most unlikely places and people, and when clues dried up, grasping at straws was a natural reaction. On the other hand, Dev was a fricking ghost hunter. Was the New Orleans Police Department actually using psychics and mediums to solve their cases now? Then again, what did I care? If it worked, that's all that mattered. I might have even entertained employing some if I knew it would help me solve Reagan's case. Maybe.

Detective Miller finished what she was doing and passed me a typed statement to sign. As I did that, she went to photocopy my file on Dustin that I'd luckily had in my purse, and then came back to return the originals to me, Dev on her heels.

"Hey, how are you holding up?" Dev asked, placing a hand on the back of my chair.

"Fine. Just exhausted," I answered truthfully. I stood and faced him, taking in his Caribbean blue eyes that looked a little tired, as well. I turned to Detective Miller. "Are we finished?" I asked, hoping the answer was yes.

"You are," she said, and I almost sighed in relief. "We have your contact information—both of you,"— she faced Dev for a second—"and we'll call if anything happens or if we need anything else."

"Is there any way you can keep me abreast of the progress?" I asked. "I know I don't really have that kind of clearance, but I have to go back and tell my client that his quarry is dead. And not just dead . . .

murdered. He's probably going to be pissed that I'm keeping the deposit."

She smiled. "I'll see what I can do." She turned to face Dev again. "Nice to see you again, Dev. Tell your grandma hi for me, and thank her for the muffins she sent over last month."

Dev flashed her that smile that made my knees weak. "Will do, Stephanie."

Dev and I walked outside and took the steps down to Broad Avenue. I saw him glancing behind me a few times with a strange look on his face and shifted to see what had caught his attention, but I didn't see anything. When I turned to face him again, he looked a little nervous. "What's up?"

"Nothing," he said with a sigh. "Just tired, I guess."

I wasn't sure I believed him, at least, not entirely, but I wouldn't push. I really was exhausted, too. This had been one hell of a first day back in my old haunts —no pun intended.

I shivered a little from the chill in the air, and Dev reached out and rubbed my jacket-covered arms. Normally, I wasn't a touchy-feely person and usually shied away from uninvited contact. Even going so far as to call out people who touched me too familiarly and without consent. But something about Dev made me hold in those words. Both earlier and now, despite my body's natural knee-jerk reactions. Because I didn't *want* him to stop, I realized. That wasn't something I'd ever felt before, and I didn't know how to process it. I wasn't sure if it was the excitement, the fatigue, or just Dev. I decided not to dwell on it too much. It really wasn't important . . . the whys of it. We had chemistry, there was no denying that, and I would let it unfold as it would. If it did . . .

"I should head back to the hotel," I said and stuffed my hands into my pockets.

"And I should get home. I have about a dozen missed calls and texts from the team, and still need to do some research on the history of Arborwood before we really get started. Will you be okay making your way to The Ravisan alone?" he asked.

"Yeah, I'll be fine." I pulled out my phone. "Just a couple of taps and I'll have a rideshare whisk me away."

He waved his cell. "Same. But I need to run into the all-night market for a couple of things first. I never did finish my errand when I ran into you earlier." He smiled.

"Oh my gosh, I'm so sorry," I said, honestly feeling bad for derailing his afternoon. Though the deviation had been his idea, so I probably shouldn't feel too badly.

"No worries at all. An afternoon and evening in your company was better than any trip to the food shop—despite how our night ended. I'll call you tomorrow and we can set up a time to meet at the property for the walk-through. I'd like you to show me around before I let the rest of the team in. Is that okay?"

"Sounds great. But can I ask a favor?"

"Anything," he said, and I truly believed he meant it. I wasn't sure what to do with that.

"Can we not do it until after noon?" I chuckled. "I'm not the best morning person, and I'm absolutely drained right now."

"I promise not to call you until at least twelve-fifteen." He tucked a piece of hair behind my ear, and I shivered. The reaction had absolutely nothing to do with the cold this time. "Goodnight, Hanlen. May your dreams guide you to the answers you seek." And with that, he turned on his heel and walked away, and I set up my ride back to The Ravisan, wondering exactly what kind of dreams I would have. I had a feeling they'd feature a certain man with rich, walnut skin and extraordinary eyes the color of the beach vacation I never let myself take.

Chapter 7

Dev

I watched from around the corner as Hanlen got into a silver Camry and rode away in the direction of her hotel. Once she was gone, I sent a quick text to the number she'd called me on earlier, asking her to let me know that she'd made it to The Ravisan safely, and then went to find the people who had gotten my attention when Hanlen and I exited the police station.

When I crossed the street and entered the little open area that people used to walk their dogs, I saw them up ahead, on a bench under a live oak. When I approached, the male stood and helped the female up.

"Hey, Dev." Findley McNair was dressed for a

summer day in New Orleans, but despite the uptick in wind whipping my curls about my head, his hair remained in perfect, artful spikes as his dark eyes took me in.

"Hey, Fin," I replied. "How are you guys doing?" I took in the beautiful woman at his side and felt a pang in my chest. Her long, silky twists fell perfectly around her bare shoulders, her arm tightening around Fin's waist as she leaned into his side.

"We're fine, brother," she said. The look in her flashing green eyes and the sound of her voice nearly made my heart break. I had lost Wren almost two years ago now. She had been found in a little grove of trees in one of the smaller cemeteries, her throat slit, her body posed, and a copper token left on her forehead—just like Dustin Reynolds. The night Findley found her, he joined her in the great beyond, the victim of a senseless accident, the result of him being distracted by his grief. The only saving grace was that they still had each other, and they seemed to rather like their otherworldly existence, playing Nancy Drew and Joe Hardy.

That didn't mean I didn't miss my sister and her great guy with a fierceness that sometimes took my breath away. Just because I could still see and talk to them didn't mean I didn't ache to grab them both in a huge hug.

I sometimes wondered if I was the reason they were still on this plane. In my grief, I had done a séance to try and speak to Wren after her murder, and it was brilliantly successful, even though she never actually saw her attacker. Unfortunately, as I found out later, it had resulted in Wren disappearing for a bit from Findley's side. They eventually found each other again, and neither had seen the light nor felt the pull to leave just yet. As long as they had each other, and I knew they were safe and happy, I would be selfish and soak up as much time as I could with them, however I could. And I couldn't lie, they *really* helped with the show. Still, I had a feeling that whenever we solved Wren's murder and caught the person responsible—and I was convinced that we would eventually —they may both disappear from my life forever. I wasn't sure how I felt about that. But I would face that possibility when and if the day ever came.

"So, it looks like we have another RƎDRΩM case on our hands, huh?" Findley said.

I shook my head. It was so stupid. Not only did this sadistic, psychopathic bastard leave his little copper tokens on his victims' foreheads, but he'd also signed his single taunting piece of correspondence to the police and the press: RƎDRΩM after Wren's murder. Redrum, like in *The Shining*, but with some twists. Murder backwards, the scruple and the omega adding a bit of narcissistic flair. We had a feeling it might be an anagram or a cipher or something, but we couldn't figure it out—and neither could the cops. The only things we knew were the factual pieces: the murder reference, the fact that a scruple was both a measure of weight and a sense of right and wrong, and that the omega denoted a last, final, ultimate end.

Not ominous at all.

I sighed. "Looks like," I replied, watching my sister's face for any signs of distress.

"Desmond told us what happened," she said. "We didn't get there until later."

"Desmond, the soldier?" I asked. The ghost was a relic from the War of 1812, and one of my best runners. He was an invaluable go-between in the spirit world on investigations, ferrying messages for me so we could get to the bottom of things quicker.

"Yes," Fin acknowledged. "Everything was the same. The modus operandi, the signature. But again, why? The Akashic Records tell us that this guy was just some ex-con skipping out on parole and engaging in petty theft along the way. And he was locked up for nearly twenty years prior to a couple of months ago. Why would this serial killer target him out of all the people in New Orleans and the surrounding parishes? But then again, why would he target anyone he killed?" He pulled Wren to him, kissing the top of her head.

"Why, indeed? I'll see if I can make contact with this Dustin Reynolds later to perhaps get some of the answers we're missing. Fill in some of those pieces. Have you guys discovered anything else of use?"

Wren shrugged. "Sadly, not really. But I do have a question."

"What's that?" I asked.

"Who was the woman you were talking to earlier?" She smiled, a twinkle in her otherworldly, faded-dollar-bill eyes. "She's pretty."

My sibling may be on the other side of the veil and only five minutes younger than me, but she could still *little sister* with the best of them, sticking her nose into my business every chance she got. It made something twinge in my chest—thoughts of all the things we had and would miss out on in life. But I forced a smile and answered anyway. "The owner of the plantation we're doing our next show on. Hanlen Arbor. And, ironically, the private investigator assigned to hunt down our newest deceased and bring him back to his parole officer in Texas, despite how that worked out. But, yeah, she's not bad on the eyes." I grinned.

"But . . ." Fin said.

I shook my head. "But nothing. She's beautiful. Inside and out, from what I can tell. Though there's pain there, too. A story I haven't heard yet, but hope to. Something broke her, that much is clear, and she's still trying to pick up those pieces."

"You liiiike her," my sister singsonged.

"If I could give you a noogie right now, I so would. And maybe throw you in a closet." I laughed, and she did, too.

"Just razzing you, big brother," she said and snuggled closer to Fin. "We'll keep looking and report back anything we find. You do the same. You know how to reach us. Do you need help with this next case?"

"I'm not sure yet. I'm supposed to get the lowdown on the property from Hanlen tomorrow before I fill in the team and get busy setting things up. I actually have very little information on what kinds of sightings and experiences have been going on there, or the down-and-dirty history of the place. We just reached out because of all the chatter on the rental site and because it's a place I've eyed for years. The next few days will be full of a bunch of research."

"You like it. You always were a nerd," Wren teased.

"Intellectual badass, thank you very much." I winked.

"Get home safely," Findley said, and my stomach did a little flip. He said that every time we parted ways, and he likely always would.

"Will do," I assured. "Take care of each other."

I heard a stereo, echoed, "Always," as they turned and walked away, hand-in-hand, disappearing from sight like fog burning off in sunlight. Time to get home and do some internet searches and think about possibly reaching out to our dead ex-con.

My phone dinged, and I looked at the screen.

Hanlen: *Tucked safely away. Thanks for keeping me*

company today. It was nice, despite how the night ended. Talk to you tomorrow.

I sent back a quick lowball glass emoji, knowing she would likely crack open one of her whiskey bottles tonight, especially after the events of earlier, followed by a sleepy-faced emoji and a thumbs-up.

It had been a while since I'd been excited about meeting with a client for a walk-through. But this time, it had nothing to do with the locale and everything to do with the woman with eyes the color of her favorite beverage and hair like sun-kissed silk.

Maybe contacting Dustin could wait. Or maybe it didn't matter. I had better thoughts to occupy my nighttime hours.

Chapter 8

Hanlen

I woke earlier than my alarm, excited to see Dev again, only to be disappointed. He called at twelve-fifteen on the dot as promised, but only to say that he couldn't get to the property today. Apparently, he had a bunch of research to catch up on that he couldn't do any other time, and some eyewitnesses to interview. He asked if we could meet tomorrow for the walk-through instead. I didn't mind. Not really. I had some work to do as well, and I took a few hours to walk the city, taking in the sights and smells and reminiscing about my days with Reagan. But as the day wore on, I found myself missing Dev. Which wasn't something I wanted to analyze too greatly quite yet.

Content from my long yet enjoyable day, I settled into the couch in my room, a glass of apple whiskey and ginger ale in my hand, my thoughts going in a million different directions. I still couldn't believe my mark was dead. And not just dead, but brutally murdered. The thought of seeing his body in that copse of trees threatened to bring back memories of things I would just as soon forget. I had pulled some strings and obtained the crime scene photos from Reagan's murder, and the images were startlingly similar. There hadn't been a coin or token left on or by Reagan's body, but she had been mostly exsanguinated and then left to fade in that dirty alley. No other clues. No fibers or hairs or fingerprints or DNA. No shoe prints or tire tracks. Just my best friend's body, cold and alone, on filthy New Orleans asphalt.

After way too many hours of senseless television and likely one too many glasses of whiskey, I glanced at the clock and saw that it was after two a.m. I really needed to get some rest. I was exhausted from the drive, the two long days, and the awful excitement of the murder. Not to mention, Dev. I didn't know why I felt so drawn to him. It had been a while since anyone had piqued my interests like that. A long, long time ago, I had once thought that maybe Reagan and I would end up together, but she had been clear that she didn't feel that way about me, and I was content having her in my life as my best friend. My person. When everything happened with her, I wondered if

I'd ever let myself open to someone again. And, truthfully, I really hadn't.

Thinking back, the last date I had been on was with an accountant from San Antonio. Someone I had met while on a case. And that was . . . wow, nearly two years ago. He and I just hadn't clicked, and like usual, I threw myself into work—and the bottle—and my obsession to get answers about Reagan. I wasn't the same person I had been back then. Far from it. And I wasn't even sure I knew all the facets of the new me. But Dev had made me forget all of that in the short time I had been with him. Something I hadn't done in far too long.

I downed the rest of my drink and went into the bathroom to rinse the glass and get ready for bed. Tugging off my shirt, my gaze snagged on the necklace I wore. I rarely took it off. It was an intricate swirling design done in bright gold, hanging from a delicate, beaded, champagne-gold chain. Reagan had owned it for as long as I could remember, but I didn't know the story behind it. All I knew was that I had found it in our little bowl by the front door when I came home from identifying her body and hadn't taken it off since. I still didn't know why *she* had removed it that night. Maybe it was her outfit, maybe something I'd never know. Whatever reason, it made me feel closer to her somehow. And, strangely, safer. I knew that was all in my head, but a person did what they had to do in the insanity that was life.

I fingered the pendant, raising it to my lips for a kiss, as I so often did. "Love you, Ray. Miss you every day." I shook my head to clear the tears threatening and finished my nightly routine.

When I slipped between the cool sheets, I initially thought there was no way I'd be able to rest. Surprisingly, sleep quickly took me under.

I WOKE TO PANIC. I felt like I was caught in a net, struggling to breathe. Something heated my chest and neck, and I had the overwhelming feeling of being watched. When I thrashed to get free, I caught sight of a figure standing at the end of my bed, the silhouette smoky in the darkness, my eyes merely picking up the outline and no features. I pulled and wrenched some more, raising a hand to my necklace where it rested between my breasts. It was hot to the touch and very uncomfortable against my skin. I looked towards the shadow once more and saw it move, only to reveal another behind it. A scream lodged in my throat, and I fought to get up, only to tangle myself further in the net—no, wait, those were the sheets and blankets— and topple off the bed onto the hard floor. Air whooshed out of my lungs, and I took in more to yell, but the clock radio on the side of the bed turned on, stopping me. It tuned to static with noises and voices coming through. I couldn't understand what was said, but the tone and cadence were almost . . . familiar. In my sleep-hazed mind I couldn't place it, and it stopped almost as quickly as it had started. When I glanced again, the alarm display blazed a blood-red 3:33. I wondered if I had imagined the whole thing. I partially freed myself from my paltry four-hundred-thread-count cotton prison and moved for the light, only to feel the temperature in the room drop, and a whoosh of energy zip by me. The blankets flew the rest of the way off, and it stole my breath once more. *I have to be dreaming.*

"Wake up, Hanlen. Wake up!" I urged, but nothing changed. There was no way this was real. No way. Things like this only happened in the movies. I once again grasped the pendant on my chest and felt the same heat as before, only this time, the metal had an almost electric charge to it. I gasped at the goose bumps it sent skittering up my arm but gripped it tightly in my fist anyway.

"You're okay, you're fine, it's just your exhausted brain playing tricks on you. There is no such thing as ghosts. You're okay. You're fine."

I searched the room once more, seeing nothing out of the ordinary, then righted the sheets and blankets on the bed and took a shot of Evan Williams straight from the bottle before lying back down. I figured I'd be staring at the ceiling for the rest of the night. Surprisingly, the Tennessee hug of the whiskey, that comforting chest burn, lulled me, and I didn't remember anything else until my phone roused me from slumber, the sun shining brightly through the curtains I'd forgotten to shut.

I rolled over and grabbed it off the nightstand, startled to see that it was after noon. Twelve-fifteen to be exact, and the name on the readout was none other than Dev.

Well, shit.

"Arbor." I answered like I always did, feeling foolish for doing so, knowing it was Dev, and cleared my throat of the sleep frog lodged tightly in my larynx.

"Good morning," Dev said, his voice silky-smooth and intoxicating.

I cleared my throat again. "Same to you."

"Did I wake you?"

"It's fine." I yawned, my jaw cracking. "Just had a strange night full of dreams and . . . just an odd night. I guess I finally fell asleep again and my body made up its mind how much sleep it needed."

"We *did* have a pretty eventful evening the other night, and you are in a strange place."

"That's an understatement." I put the phone on speaker then stood and stretched, carrying the cell with me into the bathroom so I could peek at the damage and decide how much work I'd have to do to look human. "What's the plan for today?" I asked.

"The team and I accomplished a lot yesterday off the property, but I need to get the lay of the land at the plantation and was hoping you could tell me some of the stories *you've* heard, show me the hotspots, and fill me in on some of the history of Arborwood—both things you know are true and the possible urban legends, so I can add them to the things we're already looking into."

"Yeah, I can do that. It's all silly nonsense, but I guess that's kind of your thing."

"It's not nonsense, Hanlen. It's history. Life and death. Experiences." He was stern, but he didn't sound upset. I still felt a little bit bad about trashing his livelihood and passion.

"I'm sorry. I really am." I blew out a breath. "I think I need caffeine. I didn't mean to sound so harsh. But I made it very clear to you that I don't believe in this stuff." Memories of my dream last night—because it *had* to be a dream, right?—came back to me, and I shook my head to clear it.

"Um . . ." I looked at the time again. "I can meet you over there at two. Or, I can come and pick you up wherever you are. Whatever's easier."

"I don't have to schlep gear today. Just need to take a few notes and some pictures. It'd be great if we could ride over together. Take your time waking up and doing what you need to do. I'll text you my address and see you whenever you get here."

I yawned again. "Yeesh. Sorry. That sounds great. I hoped to salvage my hair from yesterday, but I clearly need a full—and long—shower. I feel utterly drained."

"No worries. See you soon."

"Sure thing. Bye." I tapped end on the call and stretched again, leaning in to see how bad the bags under my eyes were. My necklace fell forward a bit and I looked down, only to see a big red welt on my chest. I fingered the mark. It didn't hurt, but it was strange, and it brought back memories of the dream I'd had, and how I could have sworn my necklace had felt hot and almost electrified.

What the hell?

Chapter 9

Dev

Hanlen texted me when she arrived, and I locked up and headed down the stairs. Her SUV sat near the curb, and I saw her inside, head down, intent on her phone. I knocked a knuckle on the glass, and she unlocked the doors for me.

"Hey," I said as I slid into the leather seat.

"Hey, yourself," she replied and flashed me a smile as she locked her phone and secured it in the center nook. She still looked tired. Beautiful, but tired. I wondered how her night at The Ravisan had gone. We'd filmed a show there about a year ago, and the activity had been off the charts.

"You ready to go?" she asked. "Nothing to pick up on the way?"

I patted the backpack at my feet. "Everything I need for today is right here. Onward."

She pulled into traffic, and we headed for the highway. We didn't have to go as far as Iberville Parish, where some of the other larger plantation manors were located, but Arborwood was still about a thirty-five-minute drive. Plenty of time for me to ask some questions. Though the more I thought about it, I wanted to know more about the woman than the house. I really needed to get my head on straight. This episode was kind of a big deal—not that they all weren't. Still, the plantation was one of the oldest, and the eyewitness accounts of paranormal activity were far and wide— from family to various out-of-staters who'd come to the city on vacation and snatched up the rental for their long weekend or week-long getaways.

"So," I said, "did you and your family actually live at Arborwood?"

She glanced over at me before returning her attention to the road. "We did. I spent most of my teenage years there. We got the house from my paternal grandmother when she passed, and we lived there from the time I turned ten until I graduated from high school. And then my parents got divorced and moved away. Now, I just pay for the upkeep and hope that renters don't trash the place."

I couldn't imagine not wanting to live somewhere as grand as Arborwood. It was a stunning piece of architecture, and the history was rich. The Arbors were still known in the parish, despite none of the immediate family living in Louisiana any longer. And then there were the hauntings . . .

From what Hanlen's mother had said, there had been reports of a child apparition—which we had been unable to uncover any historical data for—the classic woman in white, a bohemian woman in long skirts and head scarves, and a ghost they called The Colonel. It would be interesting to find out if some of the things people reported were poltergeist activity— manifestations made real by the energy of a living person or persons, even from afar—residual hauntings —things that happened in the past with such energy that they continued happening in the present like echoes, or if there were real, active, and intelligent spirits in the home and on the grounds.

I turned to her. "Did you ever have any strange experiences while you lived there?" I asked.

She shook her head and rolled her eyes a bit. "You mean the bad plumbing, the ancient home settling into the swamp, and the faulty wiring? Sure, I had plenty of *experiences*."

I couldn't hold back a small laugh. "You really don't believe in any of this, do you?"

She looked at me then for a beat before refocusing on the road. "I don't mean any disrespect,

Dev, I really don't. But, no, I don't believe in ghosts."

"You will," I said and flashed her a grin.

"No, I won't. And I have my reasons."

That was interesting. She could have simply left it as a statement, that she didn't believe. But that little bit at the end piqued my interests. I wasn't sure if she'd tell me anything, but I had to ask. "Care to share?"

She took in a deep breath, and for a minute I thought she might tell me to mind my business. Instead, she surprised me. "I lost my best friend. She was taken from me, and I still have no answers, despite my best efforts. If ghosts were real, she would have found a way to reach me." She glanced at me again. "She would have told me what happened to her. We had a bond that transcended friendship or romance. Even family. She never would have just left me wondering. Never." She bit her lip.

I could *feel* the pain coming off her in waves. I knew that pain. I wasn't sure if it would help, but I felt like I needed to share a bit, as well. "I understand. My twin sister was murdered." I heard Hanlen suck in a sharp breath and saw her shut her eyes for a second. "That pain doesn't go away. It only changes. I personally find comfort in believing, but I can understand the flip-side of that coin, as well."

Saying the word *coin* made me think of Mr. Reynolds, who I had never tried to reach out to.

"Speaking of coins . . . Have you contacted your client about your dead skiptrace?"

"I did," she said. "They were kind of pissed that I got paid half of our agreed rate for basically doing nothing, but were as perplexed as I was. *Am.* Nothing that I or anybody else has dug up lends credence to a motive. He's not even from here. I assume it was just a crime of opportunity for this sicko I now know has been terrorizing the city. I mean, what else could it be, right?"

I honestly didn't know. Wren and Findley didn't seem to know, either. "That's the most logical assumption, though my intuition tells me we're missing something. But the police are being very tight-lipped, and my contacts haven't uncovered anything either."

Her brow furrowed. "Your contacts? Why would you be working on that case?"

I fiddled with a string on my jeans. Did I tell her? And if I did, how *much* should I tell her? I settled for a partial truth. "The crime—actually *all* of the murders with that signature so far—matches what was done to my sister. The person who killed your ex-con is likely the same asshole who took my family from me and murdered at least two other people that we know of so far. I personally think there are many more, but I'm not an investigator, and my investigative techniques aren't anything that would hold up in court. Me looking into it is more for my peace of mind. A search for answers of some kind, even though there is no closure for something like that. As I'm sure you know."

"I understand that," she said, her hands tightening on the steering wheel.

We both went quiet for the rest of the drive, likely thinking of those we'd lost. When Hanlen pulled up to the massive wrought-iron gate of the property, I felt a thrill skitter through me. I had wanted access to this plot of land since I pitched the idea for the show to the network, and they picked up the pilot. Now, five seasons into our tenure, we had the following, the ratings, and the clout to get into some places others hadn't been able to maneuver into as yet, and I could do the occasional episode on sites that I and the team were personally interested in, as well.

The drive was long and lined on either side by trees that created a natural tunnel of sorts, the building at the end framed beautifully as we approached. I pulled out my cell to snap some pictures through the windshield, the shadows playing beautifully over the lane and the surroundings. The house was cream and gray with forest green shutters, the columns on the front porch tall and proud. The railing around the second-story porch had been painted a burnt orange that was unusual but lent to the overall aesthetic of the property. Still, I had to joke . . .

"Did your mom pick the new colors? I feel like she's channeling her new Florida vibes."

Hanlen laughed as she pulled up alongside the front porch and turned the key. "It does look like the Miami Hurricanes threw up, doesn't it? Actually, we had a local historical society pick the colors when we updated the property. Something about it being old Southern home design and an homage to something or other. I'm not actually sure. Still, as odd as it is, it's also kind of perfect."

I had to agree. It looked wonderful, and I couldn't wait to see the inside and the acreage. Up ahead, through the middle of the property, I saw a yawning maw that reminded me of a portal. I shook myself free of an involuntary shiver when I saw an apparition pass through it. Spanish moss hung across the opening. "What's that?" I pointed.

Hanlen looked where I indicated. "There's actually a courtyard. The building is kind of a squared horseshoe shape, built around it. There are benches and a large fountain, and access to the internal balconies and a secondary access to the widow's walk. The design is quite ingenious. I remember how fun it was to play, darting in and out of the house through the open French doors to the outside and then running down the hall only to emerge through another set of doors to the courtyard. And we used to use the courtyard all the time for neighborhood and family gatherings, setting up our huge table right in the middle."

"I can't wait to see it all," I replied, mentally

imagining where we could set up the cameras and other equipment. I had barely seen anything, and this location was already a dream come true.

"Well, shall we?" she asked, and I grabbed my bag and opened the door.

"Absolutely. Let's."

Chapter 10

Hanlen

Being back at the old plantation was a bit surreal. Walking through that moss-draped arch was like taking a step back in time. I could see where the saying *ghosts of memories* came into play because I could almost see teenage me running around with my friends, especially Reagan, my mom yelling at us to be careful. Putting frogs and crawfish in the fountain and hanging Halloween décor from the balconies. They were happy memories, and I caught myself rubbing at my chest. Dev noticed.

"Are you okay?" he asked.

"I'm good. Really good, actually. Just remembering some happy times."

"Oh, that's great." He squeezed my biceps and then walked ahead, taking in the entirety of the court-yard. I could almost see him mentally taking notes and imagining things for the show. I really needed to take some time tonight and watch the clips my mom had sent. I was still way on the side of disbelief with all of it, but I knew there was an almost cult following for shows like Dev's and that a lot of people genuinely believed in it all and then some. The melting pot of life took all kinds, and those who believed in the supernatural were just another spice to the stew of it all.

Over the next hour, I showed Dev around, pointing out areas that I knew were supposed *hotspots* and telling him some stories from my childhood. He took copious notes, nodding and grinning like a fool the entire time. He really was mesmerizing. He was the kind of guy I could see myself falling for. Too bad he didn't live in Texas.

"So, my caretakers probably have better stories for you," I said, glancing at my watch. "They should actually be here in a little bit. One or both of them usually comes to the main house in the evenings. Do you want to walk the property until they show up?"

"I would love that."

We wandered around the acreage, and I showed Dev the stables and work quarters and other outbuild-ings. Most of them had been out of use for ages, but we'd had everything updated and brought to code before we left. I pointed off into the distance past a grove to where you could barely see the chimney of a home and told Dev that it was where Beatrice and August lived, and that the family cemetery was just behind it. As if I had conjured her, the woman in question came walking towards us from out of the trees, her ample grandmotherly form draped in black, her broomstick skirt stirring up dust from the path. She raised a hand and headed our way, her blue-fabric wagon trailing her like a puppy.

"Hannie girl," she beamed and pulled me in for a huge hug, wayward strands of her charcoal hair tickling my cheek. She'd always called me that, and it made me a little reminiscent, as did the gentle scent of honeysuckle that always clung to her like a second skin. "And who is this handsome fella?" she asked as she pulled back.

"Beatrice Durrand, I would like you to meet Deveraux Glapion."

"Oh, my sweet goddess. I knew I recognized you from somewhere. The host of that wonderful show. So lovely to meet you."

Dev smiled and took Bea's hand, placing a gentle kiss on her knuckles. "*Enchenté.*"

Bea fanned herself with her free hand, raising her brows at me. I knew what she meant.

"Mercy, you are a handsome one. Poor August might have a run for his money."

I swore I caught a blush creeping up Dev's neck,

but it was gone almost as quickly, and he smoothly answered, "You flatter me, but I am quite certain I could never make you as happy as he does."

Dev helped get Bea's wagon into the courtyard, and then I followed along as we walked, and she told him stories from their time on the property and the things that the renters reported to them upon dropping off the keys. I remembered some of them, but a lot were new to me, and I found myself getting sucked in. Bea had always been an amazing storyteller. I remembered her telling Reagan and me tales around campfires in the yard, relaying bits of her rich past. Bea was a bit of an eccentric, but Dev seemed to click with her. They shared the same sort of . . . energy, though I wasn't quite sure what I meant by that. When I heard them swapping recipes for gris-gris bags and witch balls—whatever the hell those were—I kind of tuned them out. I knew they were used in different religions as articles of protection, but like most other things concerning the supernatural, I didn't believe in it. I did, however, believe in the power of thought and mind over matter, so I supposed if you needed a talisman of sorts to focus those intentions, who was I to judge? I touched my pendant through my shirt, still wondering about that mark. It had faded, but it was still strange that it matched up with what I remembered of my nightmare.

The sun was just beginning to set when Dev

finally put his notebook away. "I think I got what we need for today, ladies. This has been wonderful. Thank you both for your time and great conversation."

"Oh, dear boy," Bea said and patted Dev on the cheek. "It was utterly my pleasure. And I mean that." She winked, and I laughed.

Dev sighed. "If only I were a few years older, and you weren't married," he replied and placed a kiss on her cheek, clearly making the older woman's day.

"I'd better get to my tasks, Hannie girl. August was feeling a bit under the weather today, so I left him back at the cottage to rest and then run to the store after. And I need to get a few things done before the cleaning crew comes tomorrow. So good to see you, my sweet," she said and hugged me close. "Don't be a stranger while you're in town, okay?"

I agreed, making sure to tell her to enjoy some of the vacation the show would provide the couple. She waved me off, grabbed some things, and took the steps to the second floor, headed for whatever she had on her to-do list for the evening.

"So, did you get what you needed?" I asked, turning to Dev.

"Everything and more," he said with a smile. "I have a ton of new things to do some research on, and I'll get the information off to my team to start that when we get home. Speaking of, are you ready to head out? You look beat."

He wasn't wrong. I felt utterly drained. My nearly sleepless nights were creeping up on me big time. "Yeah, let's."

We headed out the courtyard entryway and Dev stopped in his tracks. I glanced at him and then looked where his gaze was, not sure what had snagged his attention. As I did, I saw a large man walk out from around the side of the house.

"What are you doing here?" Dev asked the guy. Clearly, he knew him, which made my alarm drop a notch but not entirely.

"Oh, hey, Dev. I didn't know you would be here today. Just being proactive, is all, checking things out for wiring and whatnot."

Dev gestured for me to follow, and we met the man halfway across the drive. He was taller than average and solidly built with jet-black hair and guy-liner ringing his ice-blue eyes, his clothes a mix of punk and goth. "Hanlen, I'd like you to meet one of my crewmembers. Our tech grip extraordinaire. This is—"

The man interrupted Dev by sketching a ridiculous bow. "Remy Dee Reaume at your service, ma'am." I heard the Cajun twang in his voice and knew that he'd likely grown up in New Orleans.

Dev playfully shoved at Remy's shoulder. "Knock it off, Casanova." He grinned when Remy straightened, then raised an eyebrow and issued a whatcha-gonna-do gesture in my direction. "As I was saying,

Remy handles all our technical stuff for the show. He runs the power lines, sets the cameras, tests the audio, and hangs out in the command center during the shoots. We couldn't do a show this large without him. Seriously."

"High praise, man," Remy said. "The team actually calls me R2. Most of us have fun nicknames. Except Dev here. He's too good for that."

"Not true," Dev shot back. "Nobody's given me a good one yet."

"Oh, I'm sure I could come up with something," Remy teased.

"Nope, enough of that," Dev said. "Why are you here now?"

"As I said, just trying to get a jump. The place is big, and I needed to measure some things and map out some others. When you sent us all the address, I just figured I'd come over and take a peek around. I hope you don't mind." He turned to me.

"No, it's fine. I knew you guys were coming. So did Bea and August, even though we didn't know exactly when or how often before the filming days."

"Yeah, they buzzed me in," Remy said. "Nice couple. I parked on the road up a ways by that wayward shed."

"Oh, did you go in?" Dev asked.

"No, why?"

"Bea told me there might be some stories from out

there past the gate, some things I wanted to look into and verify, but we didn't make it out that far."

"I'll take a look on my way to the car. See if it's even feasible for us to investigate there," Remy said. "Speaking of heading out, I'm done for today, and it's getting dark. Need to head home and take care of the nightly rituals." He grinned and waved and headed off towards the gate.

"Interesting guy," I said as we climbed into the SUV. "Are all of your cast and crew like that?"

"We're a diverse bunch, that's for sure," Dev answered, buckling his seat belt. "Actually, if you're up for it, we usually have a cast and crew dinner before we start an investigation. We don't generally invite the property owners or clients, but it would be great if you came. If you want to, that is."

"That sounds wonderful. I'd love to meet your people before we delve into the show stuff."

"Awesome. I'll let you know when and where tomorrow when we finalize things."

Chapter 11

Dev

I was so damned tired. I'd stayed up way too late the night before doing all sorts of research on Arborwood and making lists for my lists. A lot went into the production of a show like this, and every episode had unique challenges. During our walk-through yesterday, I'd felt a few different things and saw a couple of others, even outside of that first apparition I'd seen crossing the courtyard threshold. Nothing major, and I didn't even let on to Hanlen that I'd seen or felt anything, but there was definite activity there, and I couldn't wait to dig in and bring it into the light.

Today, I needed to get in touch with a few of my

contacts—those alive, dead, and divine—and make sure my resources were in place. And then tonight was our pre-production cast party at Lafitte's. I couldn't wait to see Hanlen again. We'd settled into comfortable conversation on our way back to my place from Arborwood, and I found myself more and more enamored by her.

She was a unique light, and I was drawn to her like a moth to a flame. I only hoped I wouldn't get burned. Or become the gasoline to her fire. She'd been burned enough. And I knew the kind of toll that could take on a person. Not only had I lost my sister, I'd lost a dear cousin, as well. Another senseless crime in a city full of it. I loved New Orleans, and I'd never want to live anywhere else, but NOLA had its fair share of pain and heartache, and for someone who saw, felt, and lived it residually, it was sometimes a lot to take in. Especially when it hit close to home like that.

I shook away those melancholic thoughts and got back to work. I headed upstairs to my attic ritual room and opened a way, sketching a geometric veve sigil on the wooden floorboards in chalk to create a doorway to the other side before making offerings to the lwa—the primary spirits of Vodou—and inviting the others in that I wanted to talk to. About an hour later, I had secured the assistance of Maman Brigitte, lwa of the dead; my runner ghost, Desmond; Fin and

Wren, of course, and a few other dearly departed I used as scouts. I had done a ritual the other day to protect everybody, including Hanlen, from anything or anybody that might mean them harm or set out to hurt them. I always did it as a precaution before a hunt got underway. There was even a paragraph in the client contracts that gave me permission. It was just worded in such a way that those who didn't believe wouldn't be alarmed by it and wouldn't think anything of it.

Just as I was closing the way and shutting the metaphysical door to the other side, my cell rang. It was one of my co-hosts.

"Hey, Lark," I answered. "What's up?" Larken Maynard, better known as *Birdie* to most of the cast and crew, was a powerful natural-born witch and a very strong medium. She was highly sensitive and intuitive and was an absolute gem. An amazing find for the show and for my circle of friends. We met in Jackson Square one day during my second season of *Haunted New Orleans*, our energies somehow drawn to each other. Across the way, at separate intersections, we'd locked eyes and walked towards each other, basically saying in stereo that we were meant to meet. She had been new to the city and down on her luck at the time, living out of a local shelter and looking for work, and things were getting big enough with the show that I really needed a co-host. Two episodes later, we introduced her to the world as a paranormal investigative trainee and the rest, as they say, is history. I couldn't imagine the show without her—or the rest of my team, honestly.

"Hey, Dev. Say, this is really random, I know, but Gunnie came to me last night."

I felt a bit of a shiver at the name. I hadn't talked to my cousin in some time. She was what I liked to call a shy ghost. She still hadn't moved on, as often happened with most dearly departed who'd been taken suddenly and tragically, but she didn't like to be super active on this side of the veil either. I saw her occasionally and knew she was okay, but it still pained me greatly that her murderer hadn't been brought to justice.

"Yeah," I said hesitantly. "What did she have to say?"

"That's just it. I'm not sure. I felt her, heard her, and sensed her urgency, got the random impressions that came with her visit, but it was almost like she was . . . underwater, for lack of a better description. I couldn't really understand what she was trying to tell me. It was kind of like something was blocking her. I just wanted you to know. I'm not sure why she didn't come to you directly, but I thought you should know in case you wanted to try and reach out."

"Thanks, I appreciate it. Are you coming tonight?"

"Wouldn't miss it for the world," she said, and I heard the smile in her voice. "I gotta run. I have a hair appointment before I need to get ready for later. Talk soon."

"Bye." I disconnected the call and thought about Gunnie. Why would she go to Lark and not me? If she had something to say, I was always a safe place. I'd have to think about it later. I had to do some research at the local library and run a couple of errands to pick up some new equipment, and the day was already farther along than I'd like.

———

AT SEVEN ON THE DOT, my phone buzzed with a text.

Hanlen: *I'm downstairs.*

Me: *Why don't you come on up for a second? I'll buzz you in.*

Hanlen: *K.*

A couple of minutes later, presumably after she'd parked, the chime sounded from outside, and I hit the buzzer to unlock the security door and finished what I had been doing. When footsteps sounded on the stairs, I called out.

"Up here."

I glanced up when Hanlen rounded the landing, and my heart nearly stopped. She was gorgeous in some kind of black and cream bustier and a leather jacket, paired with black jeans and knee-high boots. She looked incredible.

"Wow," I said, trying to unstick my tongue from the roof of my mouth.

She spun, actually looking behind her, and I had to laugh. "You, Hanlen. *You* are wow. You look amazing." Her beautiful skin pinkened with a blush and it made me smile wider. She had no idea how alluring she was.

"Thanks. You don't look so bad yourself." I peeked down at one of my favorite outfits, a fitted band tee and ripped-knee jeans, my Doc Martens the only thing that actually cost any money. But if she liked it, who was I to say she was wrong?

"Thanks." I returned to what I had been doing. "I'll just be a minute. Have to feed the beast."

She cocked her head and raised a brow, making me smile. In answer, I opened the door to the room next to me and my blue nose pit bull came bounding out, her little tail wagging a million miles an hour as she spun in circles in the kitchen, completely oblivious to the fact that we had company. She was too excited for her dinner.

"Oh my God. She's precious." Hanlen dropped to her haunches, and my baby girl finally caught the woman's crisp eucalyptus scent. The hair along the ridge of her back stood up a bit and she stopped, staring at Hanlen as her nose worked the air.

"It's okay, Mystique. She won't hurt you. Go say hello. Hanlen's a friend." I patted her on the rump.

Hanlen held out her arms, and the dog nearly tackled her, licking her hands and her face as Hanlen gave her rubs and pats and told her she was a good girl. The sight was something to behold.

"Okay, okay," I said on a laugh and tugged my dog off Hanlen's chest. "A minute ago, you were so excited for dinner, I had to lock you in the other room as I got it ready. Now, you don't even care. Let's get some food in you. I'll have Manny come and let you out in a half-hour."

At the word *food*, Mystique perked her ears and divebombed her bowl, sending kibble flying. Hanlen and I laughed in unison as she rose from the floor and dusted off her jeans.

"She's so sweet," Hanlen said.

"Yeah, she's amazing. I rescued her from a fighting ring in the bayou. We did a show not too far from where they were holding them, and she somehow got out of the pen and ran to the set where we were setting up for the episode. She was pretty beat-up, but I immediately took her to a vet, and they made sure she was good. She found me for a reason. It was right after I lost my sister. I think we healed each other."

I looked up to see Hanlen with a hand to her chest. "That's amazing. Please tell me that you shut that place down. People who abuse animals like that deserve the harshest of punishments. Who am I kidding? I'd like to murder them."

"We absolutely busted them. I had the cops out there immediately and they were all charged, and the dogs were all taken to be treated and rehomed. From what I heard, they were all adopted. The assholes didn't even realize she had gotten away. If it weren't for Mystique, I don't know that they would have been caught—at least, not before more damage was done."

When Mystique had finished eating, she plopped down on her bed with a groan and a sigh. She always made me smile. I gave her a rub and told her to be a good girl, and as Hanlen said her goodbyes, I sent a quick text to my neighbor, asking if he could let her out in a half-hour. Like usual, he was happy to help. I'd lucked out with my neighbors. Manny and his husband ran a dog walking and mobile grooming business and were only too happy to help me with Myst when I needed it.

As we entered the SUV, Hanlen turned to me. "Wasn't this place a temple and museum at one time?"

I smiled. "One of them, yes. There are a few. There's another well-known one on Rampart Street that I'm sure you've heard of. The apartment above it is actually the site of a super tragic murder and one of the most haunted locales in the city proper." I looked over to see her rolling her eyes as I'd expected. It only made me grin harder. "But . . . yes. The downstairs of this building used to be the Laveau Museum. There was a fire about eight years ago, and it's been shut down since. I had it fixed up and use it mostly for storage now. And occasionally as a headquarters for the cast and crew. There's office furniture, computer equipment, and some other things in there."

"Wow," she said, seeming impressed. "That's huge. How in the world did you end up acquiring a property like that? Do you live there alone? I think I remember hearing that it's been in the Laveau line for over a hundred years."

I was shocked. I had assumed she knew my history. Nearly everybody put two and two together when they heard my last name. And I couldn't help but feel that maybe she was fishing for some personal information, too. That made something inside me warm. "It's just Myst and me." I waited a second and let that sink in and then continued. "It's family land and holdings." I paused for another beat, but she just pulled out into traffic.

"Marie Laveau had seven children, only two of which lived. One of the two surviving daughters, her namesake, Marie Catherine Laveau, entered into a domestic partnership with a nobleman of French descent, and they, in turn, had fifteen children. Her common-law husband's name was Christophe Dominick Duminy de Glapion." I glanced at her and watched as it sank in.

"Holy crap, Dev. You're a Laveau?"

"Glapion." I smiled. "But, yes, I am. Fourth-generation."

"Just . . . wow," she said. "Okay, I kind of get some things about you now." She glanced at me again. "You know I don't really believe in this stuff, but the history of the Maries and their offspring is vast and varied. And some of the things recorded were irrefutably proven without logical explanation." She shot me a smile. "I promise to be more respectful. You're like . . . New Orleans royalty."

I laughed. "You don't have to worry about that. You're fine."

Hanlen pulled into the lot at Lafitte's Blacksmith Shop and parked around the back. Lafitte's was another of New Orleans' hotspots for both tourists and locals alike. Not only one of the oldest buildings in the French Quarter but also—reportedly—one of the most haunted. And I could attest to the fact that they weren't only stories.

Most hauntings presented as mist and shadow. One of the main apparitions at Lafitte's, the one said to be Jean Lafitte himself, showed himself to me as a full body rendering in full-on sailor's gear. And he was a salty, foul-mouthed, trickster bastard. I'd also had run-ins with a woman on the second floor a time or two. She was always a bit shy, but when she finally decided to make herself known, she could talk your ear off if you let her. When we did our show there two seasons ago, we captured the electronic voice phenomenon footage to prove it. But outside of the ghosts themselves, there were rampant reportings of other occurrences—electronics dying spontaneously, jewelry mysteriously falling off, watches being wound, ghostly red eyes being reflected in the mirror behind the booth at the back, plants in the courtyard reaching out to grab patrons. It might be an interesting evening with all of us in there tonight.

"Have you ever been here?" I asked Hanlen as we walked around to the front.

"Once, but not for long. I stopped in one Halloween for a drink with some friends."

"Anything strange happen?"

She looked at me. "What? Like ghosty stuff?" I nodded. "My cell phone died so I couldn't call for a ride home, and I lost my wrap bracelet. That's about all that happened. I was kind of pissed, truth be told."

I laughed. "You do realize that those are a couple of the things that most people who experience the paranormal activity in the bar report, right?"

"Yeah, yeah. I know. Doesn't mean it's real." She flashed me a grin that made me want to kiss it off her face.

Whoa, Dev. Slow your roll. You just met her, and you don't even know anything about her love-life situation yet.

We rounded the corner, and I saw some of the crew at the tiny metal tables and chairs in the minuscule garden courtyard to the side of the building. Lafitte's was pretty small all around, but they somehow packed a ton of people in there each night, and it never felt overwhelming. I figured it must be the magic of the place.

"There's some of the gang now." I pointed, and Hanlen followed my finger to the group of four at the table.

"I'm strangely nervous," Hanlen said with a small laugh.

"You shouldn't be." I bumped her shoulder with mine. "They're all great people and they will be basically living in your house for a couple of days.

"All right, let's go meet the uninvited houseguests."

I laughed and we made our way through the tiny swinging gate and to the table. Everybody stood with smiles.

"Okay," I started. "Guys, this is Hanlen Arbor, our gracious host for the next several days." Hanlen gave a shy little wave and then stuck her hands into her pockets. I smiled down at her.

"This motley crew from left to right is Schuyler Liu, our amazing forensics expert." The petite, dark-haired beauty waved and ran a hand through her raven-wing hair, her full finger ring getting caught in the locks. She had her dark eyes done up with both black and white eyeliner tonight.

"You can call me Sky," she said.

I moved on. "Paxton Chase, who is actually an excommunicated priest—a story I'll let him tell you later if you both want. We call him Padre. He handles all of our suspected dark activity." The blond reached out and offered Hanlen a hand.

"Larken Maynard, my super talented co-host, who you will hear called Birdie by just about everybody—except for me. I usually call her Lark." The redhead saluted with two fingers, a newly hair-dressed curl dropping over her forehead.

"And you've met R2, our Jack-of-all-trades." Remy sketched a bow again, and Hanlen shook her head with a laugh.

Everybody moved over and made room for us, pulling up a missing chair. Hanlen and I sat. "Where are Van, Halen, and Harper?" I asked.

Lark looked at the building. "Inside, getting drinks. They just got here." She raised her glass of wine and took a sip.

"Wait," Hanlen said. "Van and Halen? Are those nicknames?"

I chuckled. "Nope. Those are their given names. Van and Halen Arnot. Brother and sister. Their parents were huge fans. The team calls them the super twins. Van's a ridiculous electrical engineer and builds a lot of our tools, and Lennie is a computer engineer who creates the kickass apps to go with them."

"Wow," Hanlen said, a bit of awe in her tone. "I feel like I'm saying that word a lot." She laughed. "You guys really do have it all on this team."

"There are even more that I use from time to time for special things, but this is our core crew."

Sky reached out and touched Hanlen briefly on the arm. "But we don't all believe in this malarkey. I find great pleasure in debunking these stories, if you want the truth. But it's an amazing show and a great team. Harper agrees with me. She's a licensed psychologist. Every time we get a supposed possession case, we just look at each other and roll our eyes. But she's amazing at calming our worried and sometimes traumatized clients."

"Hey, don't dismiss it all offhand. I have intimate knowledge of demonic activity and dark hauntings," Padre said and raised a brow at Schuyler.

"So you say," she said with a quirk of her lips just as two women—one brunette and one blonde—and a tall, tawny-haired man walked towards us from inside.

"Hey, guys," I said, standing to give Lennie and Harper hugs and fist-bumping Van. "So, the gang's all here. Hanlen, this is Van, Halen, and Harper." They all exchanged hellos and handshakes. "Now, do you want something to drink?"

She seemed to think about it for a minute. "Can you get me a Zombie Killer?"

I raised a brow. "No whiskey tonight?"

"A girl can be impetuous. Cider sounds good."

"Done." I squeezed her shoulder before walking into the establishment and up to the bar. I looked around at the patrons, seeing a few that I knew. The most well-known New Orleans Voodoo Mambo sat in a corner with a man. One of my previous clients sat on the other side of the place, raising a beer in my direction. I waved. Just as I was about to take my turn with the bartender, another familiar face appeared from the restroom area. He walked towards me, his surfer-boy good looks disarming, especially paired with the wire-rimmed glasses he favored. Burke was my newest member. The team hadn't even met him yet. I hoped they would all get along.

"Hey, man. So glad you could come," I said and clasped palms, giving him a bro-hug. "Are you ready to meet the client and the crew?"

"Very. I hope they like me," he said and ducked his head.

"They will. What are you drinking?"

"Can you get me a Bud Light? Here's some cash." He dug into his pocket, but I stopped him.

"I got it. Welcome to the brood."

We took the drinks back outside and approached the table. "So, guys, I've noticed we've been struggling a bit with the research side of things lately. You all have lives outside of the show, and I respect that. I don't want any of us hitting the burnout stages or overworking ourselves. So, I hired us some help. I'd like to introduce you all to Burke Mathers. He's a web sleuth and local historian who does some temp teaching at LSU a couple of times a month. I already used him to verify some things for Arborwood, and I hope we can use him more as the series progresses."

"Bless you, Dev," Harper said and looked at Burke. "Welcome to the team. The big guy often has me doing a lot of the research, but I usually just end up wanting one of the super twins to write code to do the web scrubs for me." She laughed.

"I'm happy to help. Celebrated nerd and lover of all things true crime, historical, and supernatural. This is kind of a dream job." He laughed. It sounded a little nervous, but I imagined that this would work out well.

Though they didn't say anything, Remy and Van looked a little strained, strange expressions on their faces. Neither was big on change. Anytime we brought someone new on or changed up something about the show's processes and procedures, they balked a little. Neither ever gave me any guff, given I was the mastermind behind the show and technically their boss, but there was always a noticeable shift in their attitudes. Like tonight. But I decided to let it go for now. If anything happened, I'd handle it.

The ladies were clearly enamored by Burke. He was charming and funny and had us all laughing well into the night. I even saw the guys joining in. This would be good for the team.

I glanced at Hanlen, making sure she was okay. She'd been laughing and joking and trading stories with everyone. Flirting with me. I had snuck some casual touches, reveling in the electricity that always seemed to exist between us and the satisfaction of having her touch me in return. It was nice. She seemed so . . . light tonight. And I got the answer I had been wanting, too. Someone—maybe Lark?—had asked her if she was married, and she had said that she wasn't, and wasn't dating either. That was great news for me. I wanted to see more of her during this trip. Yes, it was a job, but she was a captivating woman, and I wanted to get to know her better.

Later, Padre and I got up to get another round for everybody, and R2 and the super twins left, all of them having early mornings. I wouldn't have to be out at the plantation until the afternoon, after their initial work was done. While Padre waited for the bartender to fill the order, I took the back hallway to the bathrooms. As I was glancing at my phone, I bumped into someone, only to have the newly familiar scent of eucalyptus wash over me.

Hanlen.

"We need to stop meeting this way, Mr. Glapion," she said, her eyes a little sleepy, her posture relaxed.

"I don't know," I replied. "I kind of like it."

She leaned a shoulder against the wall next to me. "You do, huh?"

"I do." I tucked a strand of hair behind her ear. "Having fun?"

She smiled lazily. "I am. Your friends are great."

"They can be your friends, too."

"I may just take you up on that offer. Does that mean that you're my friend, Dev?" Her gaze roamed my face, and I felt it in parts south of the border. Damn, she was potent.

"I'd love to be your friend."

"I'd like that, too. The thing is, I think friends should help each other out."

"I agree. What did you have in mind?"

"I've been doing some thinking. I think it would be really great to kiss you. Like . . . really great."

I tried so hard to suppress the smile. Yes, she was definitely tipsy, maybe even a bit drunk, but I imagined this was probably incredibly serious for her, too. Especially given her losses and the fact that she hadn't been with anyone in a while as she'd told the girls. "I would be amenable to that," I teased.

"You would?" she asked, seeming surprised. Did she not realize how beautiful and captivating she was? Had our shameless flirting outside not tipped her off to the fact that I was more than interested?

"How's this for an answer?" I reached down and palmed the nape of her neck under the silky fall of her hair, my thumb caressing her cheek as I urged her head back. She rose on tiptoe to reach me, and our lips met in an indescribable melding of desire. Yet there was care there, too. On both sides. It was . . . everything. We gave. We took. We shared breaths. And I felt as if she reached my soul.

She dropped flat to her feet and took a small step

back, placing her fingers over her kiss-swollen mouth. "Wow."

"Wow, indeed." It was all the answer I could give.

I was officially a goner for Hanlen Arbor.

The time we had for the show wouldn't be nearly enough time in her company. And the next day without her as she did some work, and I did what I needed to do for the shoot, would be hell.

Chapter 12

"It was night, and the rain fell; and falling, it was rain, but, having fallen, it was blood."
~Edgar Allan Poe

Darkness always brought with it a calming sense of serenity, a cloak of rightness that rested on the shoulders like a comforting weight. Yet, with that velvet hug came a gnawing hunger. A need to sate the desires of a dark soul. Tonight, was one of those nights.

With eagle eyes, he watched his prey through the windows of the dimly lit building, moving slowly, struggling, nearly begging for relief. This was a kindness. An act of mercy. A good deed for not only himself but many—his target, their struggling loved ones, those with no time to help . . .

It was a completion of the circle—eternal life for both him and his chosen—though in vastly different ways.

He'd watched this quarry for a couple of nights now, taking in their habits, their defenses. He didn't always do this. Sometimes, the darker side of him demanded instant gratification, and he acted on impulse like he had in the park with the motorcycle man, instinct driving him to choose. With this one, he'd nearly approached the night before, but something in his gut had told him that it wasn't the time. Not yet. Now, however, the *other* inside of him demanded satiety, and he was helpless to refuse.

Go. Take. Claim what is offered. What is yours to possess.

The symphony of midnight washed over him, and a frisson of awareness skittered over his skin, dumping adrenaline into his veins better than any hit—even of the finest drug.

When his intended opened the door and moved into the yard, as they did every night around this time, he felt another surge of excitement, almost sexual in nature, and sucked in a shallow breath. How fortunate this quarry was to have been selected. What an honor to serve.

Distracted and intent on their nightly chores, his offering was caught completely unawares by the first flash of silver in the moonlight, rendering them malleable in seconds, severing the spine in such a way that it killed feeling but kept the blood pumping. He gently lowered them to the ground, careful to pay the proper respect. He was ready. Prepared. He had done this several times now and had a system, only getting better with each offering made.

Brushing a gloved palm over a face so full of emotion and . . . *life,* it brought forth tears and a surge of gratitude, almost enough to feed the demon within —almost, but not quite.

"Thank you," he whispered.

He made quick work of freeing the life-giving elixir from its vessel, using tools of his unique design, and then taking it into himself while still hot, feeling the rush of life and strength and vitality it offered. It untethered both himself and his intended from the crippling grip of sickness. When he finished, he dropped his head back with a groan, the silky glide of pure mortality escaping to dribble down his chin.

The darkness within him purred in delight.

As quickly as possible, he gathered what remained of his sacrifice's offerings to take with him, ensuring that he staged the scene, said a proper prayer to his unholy patron, and left a coin for Charon to ferry them across the River Styx.

His donor was now free of their earthly tethers and on the way to Paradise. He wouldn't leave them stranded on the bank.

He wasn't a monster, after all.

Chapter 13

Hanlen

I hadn't gotten nearly enough done yesterday despite ordering delivery and not even showering or getting out of bed. I'd camped out on the mattress with my tablet and laptop but didn't even make a dent in what I'd hoped to accomplish. My mind was all over the place. Yes, Dustin was no longer my concern, but I had a ton of other casework to deal with. Things I could do remotely and virtually. That had been my caveat to my mother. That I would come and oversee the show's happenings and make sure the plantation was looked after, but that I still needed to do my job. Granted, that had all been before Dustin Reynolds' murder, and even more so before meeting Deveraux Glapion.

The man consumed my nearly every thought now, and it was utterly disconcerting. And that kiss at Lafitte's . . . oh my God, that kiss. It didn't help. It was unlike anything I'd ever experienced before, and it wasn't something I would likely forget anytime soon. I had been just drunk enough not to care. To throw caution to the wind and tell him what I wanted. And he had delivered spectacularly. I had no idea what it meant or what the rest of this trip or beyond would hold, but I decided I deserved a little happiness in the shitshow of my life. We'd texted several times yesterday, and every time the phone dinged with a new message, I felt a smile overtake my face. It'd been a long time since I'd smiled like that, for no huge reason. And it felt wonderful. But that didn't help my concentration.

It also didn't help that I hadn't been sleeping worth a damn outside of thoughts of Dev, either. Dreams like the one early in the trip, of the figures in my hotel room, kept replaying, making me a little bit crazy. I knew it was simply a byproduct of what I had been immersed in since arriving back in Louisiana, but it was still annoying. Every time it happened, I woke feeling a strange sense of urgency that I couldn't place. As if I should know something and do something about it. But I couldn't pinpoint it.

Last night's had been particularly brutal. I'd felt

almost attacked, the overall tone of the dream more menacing than usual. But I could glean no meaning from the bits I remembered when I woke, and I couldn't put my finger on a catalyst for why I was having these night terrors at all. I wondered if it was because I was back in New Orleans and still without any leads regarding Reagan's murder—despite me doing some digging yesterday. It was as likely an explanation as any. Sadly, I was going through my liquor stash quicker than I'd like because of it.

I was supposed to meet Dev and some of the crew at Arborwood later today. The other night at the bar had been wonderful. The cast and crew were chock-full of some really great human beings, and I actually looked forward to spending more time with them and getting to know them better.

I glanced at the alarm clock on the nightstand. It was nearing noon. I had coffee in my system, but my stomach would be grumbling for food soon, and I needed to get up and get ready to head over to the plantation.

I wrapped up what I'd been working on, saved the files, closed my laptop, and then got up to finally take a now-much-needed shower.

Turning the dial on the wall, I waited for the water to heat and stretched my tight and achy body. I knew better than to sit like that while working, but sometimes planting your butt in a nice squishy mattress was exactly what the day called for, carpel tunnel and wry neck be damned.

When I moved to shuck my nightshirt to hop into the hot spray that I couldn't wait to get lost in for a few, my heart sank. My necklace. *Reagan's* necklace. It was gone.

I frantically searched the room: in and under the bed, amidst all the bedding, in the bathroom, and near the desk. I threw on some clothes and rushed outside, thoroughly searching the SUV.

Nothing.

I couldn't hold back the tears. That was all I had left of Reagan. I needed it. I wracked my brain, trying to think of where it could be. When had I last seen it? I knew I'd had it on during the cast party—I very rarely took it off—but couldn't remember seeing it after. Though it was such a part of me that I hardly noticed it was there anymore. Maybe it was at the bar.

I flew back upstairs and grabbed my cell, Googling the number. They weren't open yet, but someone should be there. I dialed through and waited, my stomach roiling and threatening to give my whiskey from the night before a grand reappearance.

"Lafitte's, Brenda speaking."

"Oh, thank goodness. Hi, Brenda. My name is Hanlen Arbor. I was in there the night before last with a group from *Haunted New Orleans*. Unfortunately, I just realized that I lost some jewelry, and—"

She laughed, cutting me off. "If I had a dollar for every time I got a phone call like this, I'd be able to afford that penthouse apartment I want. Damn ghosts."

Her deviation threw me for a second, but it didn't matter. I continued. "Do you guys have a lost and found?"

"We sure do, sugar," she said. "What kind of piece was it and what does it look like? I'll check for you right now."

"Um . . . it's kind of hard to explain. It's a bright gold swirly geometric design pendant on a light-gold beaded chain. A necklace."

"Okay, give me a second."

I heard her set down the phone and waited with bated breath, the nausea inside me threatening to overtake me with each second that passed. After what felt like an eternity, I heard someone pick up the receiver.

"I'm holding it right now. It's safe and sound. The clasp isn't even broken. This happens so often that our regulars and staff know to snag anything they find because we all know their owners will be in touch soon."

The relief I felt nearly floored me, and I couldn't breathe for a minute, much less speak. I swallowed hard. "Oh, thank goodness. Can you hold it for me somewhere safe?"

"Of course. Come whenever you can. I'll make

sure nothing happens to it."

"Brenda, you just saved me a heart attack. Thank you so much."

"My pleasure, sugar. See you later."

I disconnected from the call and slumped down on the edge of the bed, the relief making me weak for a minute and bringing tears. I wasn't sure what I would do if I ever lost that thing. I really should look into getting a safety clasp put on it, but Brenda had said it wasn't broken, so that wouldn't have done me any good the other night.

Crisis averted and feeling the relief of knowing I'd get it back, I went to take that much-needed shower to get settled for my day.

Finally ready and out of the steamy bathroom, I grabbed my cell to see that I had three missed calls from Bea. That was strange. She rarely called me. I took a seat near the window and accessed my voice-mail. There was only one message.

"*Hannie girl*," Bea said, her voice shaky. "*I . . . you . . .*" And then she broke down in sobs.

Muffled voices sounded over the line, and then another clear voice came through. "*Ms. Arbor, this is Nurse Pritchett. I am so very sorry to tell you this, especially over voicemail, but Mr. Durrand was found dead this morning. Mrs. Durrand is in no shape to handle anything right now. I know you're not family, but we would be very grateful if you could come over to the house. I'm going to give Bea something to help her rest and will be waiting at the cottage. Thank you. And . . . I'm so sorry.*"

I couldn't believe what I'd just heard. August was dead? I needed to be there for Bea. Their only child, a daughter, had died two years ago of cancer. The sweet woman didn't have anybody else.

I made a tough call to my mother and then I called Dev.

"Hey," I said when he answered.

"Hey, yourself."

I swallowed hard. "So, um . . . I have some news. Some bad news. Bea called me when I was in the shower. They found August dead this morning. I need to go and be there with her. She doesn't have anybody else, and since I'm in town, I should go. I *want* to go. She was like a second mother to me. August was like my favorite uncle." I got a little choked up and blew out a breath to keep the tears at bay.

"Oh, Hanlen. I'm so sorry. I'm going to call the team and cancel things for today."

"No," I insisted. "Don't do that. I'll just be at the cottage. We shouldn't interrupt you guys."

"That's the least of my worries. I want to be there for you. And Bea. The show can wait. We'll be fine. The network isn't waiting on this one yet, they have plenty of cached reels to work with. And if they need to, they'll just do some reruns. We bring in enough money that they'd better not complain. I'd like to come with you. Is that okay?"

I nearly wept again, but this time from gratitude. How long had it been since I'd had someone who wanted to support me like that? To make sacrifices to make *me* happy. I couldn't even remember. Probably Reagan. She had been the absolute best support system a person could ask for. Before bad memories could overtake the good, I answered Dev.

"I'd love that, actually. I can pick you up in twenty if you're ready. Though I have to stop at the bar first before we head to Arborwood."

"Um . . . dare I ask?"

I actually chuckled when I realized how that sounded. "I lost my necklace at Lafitte's the other night. I called this morning and they're holding it for me. It's special. I'd like to have it with me. Especially today."

"Damn ghosts." He laughed. "Sorry, I shouldn't be joking. I'll be ready."

"Okay, see you in a few." I disconnected and raked a hand through my hair, tugging at the strands.

How was this happening?

Chapter 14

Dev

I met Hanlen in front of my building, not wanting to hold her up. I'd already spoken with Manny and Tristan, and they were taking Myst for a puppy spa day. She would love it and probably wouldn't even realize I was gone.

I crawled into the passenger seat and looked over at Hanlen. "How are you holding up?" I asked.

She blew out a breath and merged into traffic. "I'm still in shock, I think. I can't believe he's gone. I know that Bea said he was feeling a little under the weather the other day, but I didn't think it was bad. She even mentioned that he was supposed to go to the store."

"Do you know any details? Not that it matters . . ."

"No. Bea tried to leave me a message and couldn't get the words out. Her at-home nurse ended up leaving the voicemail. Nurse Pritchett comes every other week to check on the couple and make sure everything's good. All she said was that he was found dead."

I reached over and put my hand over hers where it rested on the gearshift, lending her a little bit of strength—both metaphorically and magically. I saw her straighten in her seat and then she turned her hand and twined her fingers with mine, squeezing a bit. She didn't let go, and neither did I.

When we got to Lafitte's, she hopped out of the SUV and ran to the front door, knocking on the side-light. A minute later, the door opened, and Brenda appeared. I watched the ladies exchange some words and then Brenda handed Hanlen a white envelope. Hanlen put her hand to her chest, cradling and hugging the paper-shrouded bundle, and said something more, but Brenda just gripped her other hand and waved her off.

When Hanlen returned to the driver's seat, her energy was lighter already. She dropped her head back on the headrest and let out a big breath. "I am so grateful that she found this," she said, shaking the envelope and making the contents rattle inside. "I don't know what I would have done without it." She tore open a corner of the paper and dropped the contents into her palm, the necklace making a golden puddle.

I moved a little closer to get a better look, and every nerve ending came alive. "Where did you get that?" I asked.

"It belonged to my best friend. It makes me feel closer to her. Makes me feel protected somehow," she said and righted the necklace. The golden veve dangled from its beaded chain, the deeper meaning of the geometric sigil representing the lwa hanging in the silence of the SUV's cab. "I know that sounds crazy, but it's always been that way."

Not crazy at all.

Did I tell her what she held? Did it matter? I decided to file the information away for later. For a better time.

I watched as she slipped the chain over her head and touched the pendant to her lips before dropping it under her shirt. I knew what I'd see if I activated my Sight. But to make sure, I did exactly that. I opened myself to see beyond the veil and clearly saw the silvery blue outline around Hanlen's aura—the protection spell woven into the piece of jewelry she wore. It was strong magic. Familiar Vodou magic. Though I had no idea what it meant. But that was for another time.

The drive to Arborwood was mostly silent, both of us lost in our own worlds, though for different reasons. When we pulled through the property gates and saw the police cruisers and ambulances and other official vehicles, I turned to Hanlen.

"That seems a bit excessive for a heart attack."

"I was just thinking the same thing," she said, driving past the main manor and getting as close to the cottage as she could.

We got out of the SUV and made our way over. Detective Stephanie Miller saw us and headed our way, stopping us before we got too close.

"What are you two doing here?" she asked, a bit of suspicion in her tone.

Hanlen made a circle with her finger, indicating everything around us. "This is my property. Bea called me this morning, and Nurse Pritchett asked me to come. I was supposed to meet Dev for some show stuff —this is their next location—and he asked to come along. He and Bea met the other day and hit it off. I thought he might be comforting to her."

"Wow, small world," Stephanie said. "I'm so sorry, Ms. Arbor. After the other night and now this . . . unfortunately, we are going to need to speak with you both again."

I saw the confusion crease Hanlen's face. "Why? I just told you my relationship and why I'm here. Not to mention, I'm not even sure why *you're* here," she said.

Stephanie appeared perplexed for a minute. "Because it's strange that two people you're associated with have now wound up dead," said another stern, male voice. I looked over to see a detective I wasn't familiar with. I thought his name was Walker or something.

"Watkins. Not now," Stephanie said and turned back to Hanlen. "Are you aware of the circumstances surrounding Mr. Durrand's death?"

Hanlen shook her head. "No, neither Bea nor the nurse said on the voicemail. I just assumed it was a sudden heart attack or something."

When I saw the look cross Stephanie's face, I knew the words that were about to come out of her mouth next.

"Ms. Arbor, Mr. Durrand was murdered. His wife thinks maybe someone followed him home from the grocery store and took him by surprise. And it seems his life was taken by the same person who killed Mr. Reynolds."

I caught Hanlen before her knees buckled.

———

A COUPLE OF HOURS LATER, after we'd made sure that Bea was okay and resting comfortably under Nurse Pritchett's able care, Hanlen and I found ourselves back at the NOPD headquarters, giving statements and answering questions once again. This time, they let us stay in the same room, though I was informed that I should only answer when addressed directly. It was difficult. Detective

Watkins seemed to enjoy playing the bad cop. I didn't like the guy and I desperately wanted to tell him off.

For someone who generally stayed pretty even-keeled and didn't like violence, my urge to give him a bloody lip was almost overwhelming. Some people just had that effect. It was an energy thing. Everything was made of spirit. And every person's aura emitted a certain kind of energy that could be felt by sensitives. It wasn't always easy to decipher because some personality traits felt similar to others and were hard to differentiate, but on the spectrum of good and bad, bad always felt . . . oily. The degree differed, of course, and it sometimes came through for things that weren't quite so serious like chronic liars and the like. But we could always tell a bad egg, unless they specifically hid it or really and truly believed that they weren't bad.

The day felt endless already. I had too much bad coffee swimming in my gut, and too many emotions roiling my insides. First the veve that Hanlen had, and then the murder. Now, watching this. They couldn't honestly believe that Hanlen had anything to do with these crimes. Could they? This was the work of a serial killer, and Hanlen had been nowhere near the state for the first several confirmed cases. Even the one the killer claimed outright with their note—my sister. But I understood their confusion, too. The last two discovered victims *had* been in Hanlen's orbit. It *was* strange, and I hoped we got to the bottom of it soon.

When they finally told us that we could go as they looked into a few things, including verification of Hanlen's whereabouts during the times of the first few murders they could attribute to RƎDRΩM, I simply held out my hand.

Without words, Hanlen fished her keys out of her purse and dropped them into my palm, and I took us safely back to The Ravisan. I helped her up the stairs and fixed her a drink, setting it in front of her.

"I'd ask how you are, but I can about guess."

She looked at me with tear-filled eyes. "What the hell is going on here, Dev?"

"I wish I knew." I tucked a chunk of silky waves behind her ear and pulled my chair close to hers so I could put my arm around her shoulders and tug her into my side. "I'm so sorry this is all happening." I kissed her hair.

She shook her head against my chest, and I felt the tension in her body. "Nobody should suffer the tragedies that you have," I said.

"Or you," she replied and looked up at me. "You lost your sister. Your twin. And even though you didn't come right out and say it, I intuited that you've lost others close to you, as well."

"I have," I confirmed. "We're quite a pair, huh?"

She quirked a sad little smile. "I think the classic

artists would have a field day with us. We're almost the epitome of a tragedy. We should get masks."

I laid my cheek on her head. "We're not doing anything with the show until this is all resolved."

She sat up and turned to me more fully. "No, Dev. This shouldn't affect that. We have a contract, and you have a job to do. I'm not sure how much help I'll be, I kind of feel like a zombie right now, but we should keep going. The cops said that the main house and the immediate area around it can be used, we just can't venture behind Bea's cabin. To the . . . to the crime scene or the cemetery." Her voice cracked, and it nearly broke my heart.

She turned to her lowball glass and knocked back her drink, pouring another and taking a small sip this time. She likely needed to calm her nerves.

"I shouldn't be drinking," she said. "I should let myself feel. But I just can't right now. I want to be numb. And I am a bit. Yet, not enough."

I grabbed her hand and rubbed the back of it with my thumb, tracing invisible veves and trying to imbue her with light and healing. I wished I had finished the gris-gris bag I had thought to make for her for protection, but I never took the time. I even had the herbs, bones, and other items sitting on the little bag in my ritual room, waiting to be assembled and spelled. At least she had the protection of her necklace, and I would do what I could outside of that.

"What can I do? What do you need from me?

Whatever it is, it's yours," I said, totally serious. I would do anything for her right now.

When she looked at me again, I immediately noticed the change. She had made some kind of decision.

"Dev?"

"Yeah," I answered, tucking that wayward lock of silky brown hair behind her ear again. The motion had become so natural. I couldn't help myself.

"Did you mean it?"

"Did I mean what?" I asked. I thought I knew what she was likely getting at, but I needed to hear her say it. Needed the words.

"That you would do or give me anything."

"Yeah, I meant it." I pulled back a bit to look at her more fully. "Why? What do you need?"

"I need you." She reached up and framed my face, bringing her lips to mine. I kissed her as I'd been starving to do since Lafitte's and put as much feeling into the action as I could. Hanlen was special. She deserved to be treated as such.

When we came up for air, I pulled back again, one hand still firmly cupped around her neck, my thumb resting in the hollow of her throat. "Hanlen, I don't want to take advantage of you. You're vulnerable right now and you may not be thinking clearly."

In answer, she rose from her chair and straddled me in mine, bringing my body to life. "I know exactly what I'm doing, Dev. I'm one-hundred-percent in my right mind right now. Am I sad? Hell, yes, I'm sad. And upset. Fucking enraged, really. But I'm also completely aware. I want you. No, I *need* you."

That was all I needed to hear. I took her lips again in a fiery kiss, letting my hands roam. She moved on my lap, nearly driving me insane. When I rose from the chair, she just wrapped herself around me, clinging tightly and never severing our connection. We touched nearly everywhere, and it was incredibly heady.

When I dropped her onto the mattress and stood back to look at her there, her hair spread around her in a fan of silk, her lips swollen and pouty, and her eyes full of lust, I had to rein myself in. She was divine. A rival to any of those I worshipped and paid homage to—no offense intended. I sent up a quick prayer to the lwas and great creator for any unintentional insult and vowed I'd give them an offering as soon as I got home. The blessings in my life right now were plenty, despite the tragedy that colored them.

I slowly stripped her, paying special attention to every inch of skin I revealed and reveling in the dips and curves of her form. There was so much strength in her body, yet she was soft in all the right places. My eyes and my hands couldn't get enough. When she was in nothing but her black and tan lace bra and panties, I stood back. She propped herself on her elbows to peer at me, and I slowly pulled off my shirt.

I heard her intake of breath and saw her pupils

dilate, and then she sat up and ran her fingertips across my skin, moving from right over my heart, across the opposite pectoral, and then back across my waist to my opposite hip.

"It's . . . I have no words," she said.

I looked down, seeing the tattoo I'd had done right after I lost Wren. It was a large albino python, its head resting over my heart, tongue tasting the world. The body ran over my shoulder and under my opposite arm, across my pec to my waist and hip, the tail dangling onto my upper thigh. It had taken nearly forty hours to complete but it was worth the pain and wait. Larken had actually helped. She'd spelled some ink so that the white and yellow would show and remain vivid on my darker skin tone, added an anti-possession and protection spell, and the artist had brought the serpent to life so vividly that he almost looked as if he were legitimately wrapped around my body and slithering across my torso. The shadows and three-dimensional realism of the snake were perfection.

"I've never seen anything like it," she whispered. "The colors are so vivid, and it's so incredibly realistic. It's a good thing I don't hate snakes." She quirked a grin at me and then swept her fingertips over the scales again, causing goose bumps to erupt across my flesh.

"It's a representation of Zombi, Marie Laveau's

pet snake. It's also one of the animals she's said to turn into now in spirit form. That, and a crow."

"How appropriate," she said and laid a gentle kiss on my navel, making me suck in a breath.

We stripped the rest of the way and took our time learning each other's bodies. I couldn't get enough of her. She was perfect, seemingly created just for me, and she tasted like the sweetest fruit, something I'd never get tired of indulging in. When I protected us, and we finally joined, I could only think that we fit like pieces of a jigsaw puzzle kept apart for a time, only to be reunited to complete a beautiful whole.

The sounds that filled the room were an erotic, musical score as we engaged in a dance as old as time. As sacred as any ritual I could complete in my temple —maybe more so. Lips and tongues and teeth, sampling, feasting. Devouring. There was a different kind of magic in this. A long-lasting, powerfully woven spell.

We shared our breaths, our bodies, our *souls* in a continued fervent frenzy of seeking hands and melded flesh. And when she arched and cried out my name for the second time, I followed her into bliss, knowing without a doubt that I wouldn't let her go without a fight. Hanlen hadn't been expected. She may have come to town amidst a flurry of death, but I knew one thing for certain: She reminded me what it was to be alive.

Chapter 15

". . . waiting in the dark, waiting, waiting . . . Maybe you can stop him. I can't."
~Dennis Rader

Shaking, sweating, he watched his newest target, planning how to execute his scheme. It hadn't been that long since he'd taken his last sacrifice and indulged in his unholy communion. The darkness inside him didn't seem to care. He felt himself fading. Knew he needed to imbibe the sacred lifeforce to renew. He was twitchy, irritable, the dark craving within him growing with each moment that passed.

This one, this prey, had been picked for an entirely different reason. He just didn't like them. There was no sexual attraction that lent itself to better sustenance like some of his earlier conquests. No good-deed goal for the greater good of the people as with the biker. No mercy like the old man. This was a bit of hatred, though that was pushing it, since he didn't care or like them enough to attach that strong of a word to it.

Maybe he'd play with this one a bit. It went against his usual ritual, but this one might deserve a little pain before death. Before they gave him what he so richly deserved and offered up their life for his.

He felt his shadow-self shimmy in agreement. Yes, he'd take his time with this one. Draw it out, add some adrenaline to the font. Perhaps that would hold him over for longer this time. Maybe that's what his sacrifices had been missing.

He looked across the way at his prey and smiled, imagining the fun to be had.

Ah, yes. Tonight would be the perfect time to start the game. The ideal time to play.

He stealthily made his way over and took them by surprise as usual, only this time he didn't eradicate the senses. He *wanted* them to feel. He merely disabled them enough that he could overpower them and take control.

When they were positioned where he needed them, he began his dance. The fear in his sacrifice's eyes was enough to give him a hard-on, but he willed it away. There were more important things to do right now. Later, he could slake his desires in another way.

He needed to be in the moment right now, and that meant staying focused and not letting his lust control him.

"Do you know how special you are to have been chosen?" he asked, flipping the copper coin through his fingers, only to return it to his palm. "To be the vessel for my continued ascension?" he went on, watching as confusion overtook his prey's expression. He almost wished he could ungag them and listen to the pointless pleading, the begging, the empty promises. But he needed to keep a low profile. This spot wasn't ideal, and there were people around.

He dropped his bag and set up his temporary altar, placing the coin in a safe place for later, and removed his ritual blade from its sheath, holding it up to see it glinting in the low light. A shiver of excitement raced down his spine, and he approached his sacrifice where they lay.

"I'm sure you're wondering why I'm doing this. You would never understand, even if I tried to explain it to you. So, instead of idle chit-chat, what do you say we just get to work, hmm?" He held up the dagger. "I think I'll start with your eyes. Eyes that looked where they shouldn't. Eyes that judged. Yes, I think we'll start there. And then . . . I will take your life. And your muffled screams will be the sweetest symphony to my feast."

Chapter 16

Hanlen

I woke to raging heat and unfamiliar surroundings. Cracking open my gritty eyes, I looked around to see a bedroom I didn't immediately recognize. Then it all caught up with me. What day it was. What'd happened the last two days. Where I was now—Dev's bedroom. And the heat was from the very sexy man snuggled against my back and the snoring canine pressed to my front. I looked down and smiled, running a hand down Mystique's silky fur. The pit bull grumbled a bit and then fell back to sleep.

I was entirely too comfortable, but my bladder waited for no man, woman, child, or adorable pup.

As gently and quietly as possible, I extricated

myself from the love sandwich and headed to the bathroom. Despite the horrific events of this trip so far, there had been a lot of good, too. And the man in the other room was directly responsible for nearly all of it. Given that we were a full day behind, we'd spent all of yesterday, from morning to the late hours of night, setting up Arborwood for the show. It was really hard work, and I couldn't believe that they did it all the time and all over the place.

Remy was constantly in motion; running here and there to make sure everything was set up properly and operating smoothly. Lennie and Van had shown me some of their gadgets and I had to admit, while I didn't believe in what they used them for, the technology behind them was ingenious. But just because they got blips on the EVP meters, it didn't mean there were ghosts. Electromagnetism existed everywhere. Still, they were really, really talented and they made things look so damn real. And Larken had displayed some things that blew my mind. *If* I believed in magic, I would think that she was made of it.

And then there was Dev. He was always so in control, knowing exactly what everyone needed before they even asked and being on top of everything. It amazed me. And like Larken, he did things that defied explanation. Again, even not believing in that stuff, I could tell that there was something special about him —with the whole team, really. And if I were honest, I found myself being opened to all sorts of things on this trip—day by day. While I had known that being back in the city would hurt—and it *did*—it also brought back a lot of wonderful memories. Things about Reagan especially that I wanted to keep alive. I didn't need to only dwell on the bad stuff. There was a ton of good, too.

I finished my business and washed my hands, taking in my reflection in the mirror above the sink. My cheeks were still a little flushed, my lips a bit bee stung. I absolutely hated the saying, but I . . . dare I say it: glowed. *Magic, indeed*. I smiled. I wasn't even crabby like usual, and it was godforsakenly early in the morning.

I grinned inwardly and opened the door to a beautiful sight. Dev sat, propped up a bit against several pillows, one knee bent and the bright white bedding pooling at his waist. He had one arm across his midsection, resting on his snake—I internally laughed at the double meaning there—the tattoo partially hidden, the other hand wrestling with Mystique as she wiggled on her back, play-grunting and trying to nip his hand. When he looked up and my eyes met those fathomless ocean-water pools, I felt it from my head to my toes. Especially in my gut. In the time I'd spent with Dev, I hadn't missed my home in Texas once. That was telling, since I never thought to return to this state, especially not this parish. And the fact that some far reaches of my mind could entertain thoughts of possibly staying because I was falling for Dev was terrifying. Things were changing so quickly, but as I gazed at the bed with Dev and the dog, I realized that the only thing that could make this better would be finding Reagan's killer and making sure they were brought to justice. Though, I had to admit, the happy memories I'd had of her while here were a bit of a balm, too.

"Come here," Dev said and held out his hand. I walked to the side of the bed and sat down. He immediately reached up and tucked a piece of hair behind my ear, flashing me one of those smiles that made me feel safe, and awakening things that should have been sated by the last couple of nights.

"It's a new day," he said, stating the obvious.

"It is," I replied, not sure where he was going with this.

"Still no regrets?"

Ah, so *that's* where he was headed. I smiled and leaned down to place a gentle kiss on his lips. "None at all. Though I do feel a little guilty celebrating life like this after just losing August."

He scooted back so he was better leaning against the headboard and could look at me more fully. "Let's not look at it that way. Let's look at it as him giving us the push required to grab what we both needed. I'm quite sure August loved you. I mean, how could someone not?" He grinned. "With that said, I think a celebration of life is exactly what he would have wanted for you. Would still want—especially given your past. This asshole plaguing the city doesn't get to take that away from everyone. Their selfishness and sickness don't get to rule. I won't let it happen."

"I wish I had your optimism," I said and leaned forward to place a sweet kiss on his chest. "And you're right. He would absolutely want me to be happy. And despite everything, in this moment, I am."

Dev grabbed my hand and kissed my fingers and then hopped out of bed, pulling me with him. "Let's get this day started, shall we?"

He spun me like a dancer, and I giggled. Actually *giggled*. What the hell?

"What's on the agenda for today?" I asked as we both threw on some clothes. The cast and crew had done *so* much already, I couldn't imagine what else there was to do before the actual shoot.

He led me to the table and pulled out a seat for me. Then he went about feeding his overly dramatic and seemingly starving dog before getting to work on breakfast for us. "We made up a lot of our lost day yesterday, but we still have some additional static trail cameras to position, hang, and test. Remy did a lot of it, but I'd like to add a few more. And some sound checks, glamour shots, filler clips, and other little things to do. Plus, I'm hoping that Burke uncovered some additional facts about the stories that I had him researching so we know where our so-called hotspots are, and I can have the gang checking for environmental reasons for those sightings and stories before we decide whether to use them for the show itself."

He placed a cup of perfectly doctored coffee and a napkin in front of me, and I inhaled the nutty aroma, sighing. "I can't believe how much goes into a show like this," I said and took a sip. "I had no idea. I just assumed you guys waltzed into a place with cameras a la *Blair Witch* and called it good." I laughed.

He kept his back to me as he tended the eggs on the stove. It reminded me of all the times I'd woken up to Reagan creating some morning culinary master-piece in the kitchen and my heart panged in response to the memory. Damn, I missed her.

"Some of the Buzzfeed and YouTube shows are like that," he answered. "But we've never been. Before I even pitched the pilot idea to the network, I knew how I wanted to do things. I think my plan was one of the reasons they decided to take a chance on yet another paranormal reality show."

"Is that an oxymoron? Paranormal reality . . ." I laughed. "But I have to say, I've been impressed. There's actually a bit of science to it all, and the tech-nology is fascinating."

He turned to me, his grin warming his eyes. "Where is my recorder when I need it? Hanlen Arbor just admitted that she's impressed by a *ghost-hunting* show. That may be more ground-breaking evidence than any phenomena my EVP recorder could capture." He winked.

I threw my balled-up napkin at him, and he ducked, chuckling as he went back to the food. "Shrink that head, Mr. Glapion. I still don't believe. And until I have proof, a skeptic I shall remain."

"Just remember, the spirits always see you. So be on your best behavior." He pointed the spatula at me. "It's when you start seeing *them* that things get really interesting."

I felt a pang in my heart, my chest tightening painfully. Despite my stance on everything Dev did, I would give anything to see Reagan again. To tell her that I missed her and that I'd always love her. Thoughts of her brought thoughts of August. I wondered how Bea was holding up. I'd have to go and check on her when we got to Arborwood.

I watched Dev for a bit as we ate, noticing that he seemed almost distracted towards the end of the meal. Myst was fast asleep in her bed, so I knew it didn't have to do with her. When he suddenly rose and put his plate in the sink, my insecurities grabbed hold.

"Did I say something wrong earlier?"

"What?" he asked, looking genuinely confused. "Oh. No, not at all. I'm sorry. I, ah, I need to make a quick phone call. Something just came to me, and I need to check it out." Without another word, he walked into the bedroom and shut the door. That was odd, because in the time I'd known him, Dev had never shut himself away while making a call.

A minute later, I heard his voice, and my curiosity got the best of me. I stood. Myst eyed me suspiciously, and I shot her a look. "Don't look at me like that," I whispered. "I'll behave. Mostly." She almost seemed to roll her light blue eyes at me and then settled back in for her nap with a grumble.

I got as close to the bedroom as I could and leaned in, catching bits of conversation that didn't make any sense out of context.

"Where? When?" Dev asked, his voice hushed. "Why isn't she coming to me? You're the second person she's gone to. No, I know it's not your fault, I'm just . . . frustrated." I heard him sigh.

"No, I haven't. Not since I spoke with them about their parts for the show. I'll have to reach out later and see if they know anything. Anything else? . . . No, I haven't heard from him either . . . No, don't worry. We'll figure it out. He's probably just busy. Thanks for letting me know." Sounds of shuffling came through the door, and I imagined Dev pacing.

"I know." I heard a smile in his voice now and wondered how the conversation had changed. "She's pretty great," he continued. "I just wish that things were easy. However, in this life, nothing ever is." He laughed. "Unfortunately, I don't think she's ready for that yet. Besides, I'm not even sure how we'd accomplish it. She's certainly not ready for an eye-opening experience of that magnitude . . . Yeah, okay, sounds good. Thanks again. I'll see you tomorrow."

The conversation ended, and I hustled back to the table as if I'd never moved, taking my last bite of eggs just as Dev reappeared.

"Everything okay?" I asked.

He had a little scowl on his face. "Yeah. At least, I think so. Just some work staff stuff. Nothing for you to worry about." He kissed me on the head as he leaned down and grabbed my now-empty plate, taking it to the sink to add to his.

An hour later, we ventured downstairs to the show's HQ and Dev initiated a Zoom meeting with some of the cast and crew. I got to meet James and Aaron, the camera operators, and a woman named Dakota that I was told was some kind of occult expert and psychic.

"Lark, I need you to establish contact with who you can today and relay our intent, and then set a circle around the property. Go as far back as the carriage house but be sure to steer clear of Bea's lot, and then come as far up front as the mailboxes. Don't worry about the shed or the cemetery," Dev said.

Larken nodded and took some notes. "Done. Where do you want the doorway so you can open the way?"

Dev looked thoughtful for a second. "I'm not sure it matters. I'll have you let us in down on the driveway and I'll sketch at the entryway of the courtyard when we begin."

I had absolutely no idea what they were talking about, but I imagined I would find out later. I wasn't ready to admit it aloud, and my stance on all things woo-woo hadn't really changed, but with each layer of the process they unveiled, the more my interests were piqued.

"Hey," Harper said. "Has anyone heard from Burke? I need him to dig into some additional things regarding the woman in the headscarves. I think I figured out who it could be, but I need someone who has more historical access."

"No," Dev said. "I checked in with him, too, and didn't get any replies. I'm sure he's just busy and will reach out later. If he's at the historical society or the library, I imagine he shut off his phone."

Paxton nodded but then cocked his head. "Where are R2 and Van?"

Dev took a drink of his water. "Remy left me a voicemail early this morning. Said he wasn't feeling well. He pretty much did everything I needed him to do already. We'll be fine without him for today and tonight, I think. Hopefully, he'll be back tomorrow. And I'm pretty sure Van was headed to Baton Rouge to pick up that new piece of equipment I am dying to try, though I'm not one-hundred-percent sure."

"Any, uh . . ." Larken started and then seemed to

glance at me through the screen, "word from our other crewmembers?"

"Nothing new," Dev said. "Not really, anyway. Desmond was doing some digging into The Colonel for us, and our favorite love birds,"—he smiled— "were asking around about the woman in white. I talked to them this morning, actually."

That must have been the call he'd made earlier. I thought back to the bits of conversation I'd overheard and wondered who else they'd been talking about— besides me. I decided it didn't matter. It was likely something I wouldn't understand anyway.

"Do you still want me to interview Mr. and Mrs. Whitaker today?" Harper asked.

"Yeah, that would be great. They had some experiences out in the side woods that I'd like to know more about. We don't have many accounts from the property, just the buildings, and it'd be good to know more so we can see if we need to look into it as possible correlating activities."

"I'm on it," she replied. "Actually, I'd better get to it. They're an hour ahead of us in Indiana. Do you need anything else right now?"

"Nope," Dev said. "Call me later or text if you need anything."

"Will do," Harper said, waved, and then disconnected.

"Okay," Dev said. "Hopefully, Burke's looking into our bohemian ghost, Harper's interviewing the

Whitakers, and Lark's getting Arborwood ready. Sky, Padre, I won't need you guys today I don't think, so why don't you two go and do a preliminary check on our next property since we'll need to jump into that the minute this one's a wrap?"

"Yeah, we can do that," Schuyler answered, and Paxton nodded.

"James, Aaron, I need you guys to do a bunch of glamour shots and things first thing today. Get some low footage of the house through the woods. Some traveling reels coming up the driveway. If you have time, can you send up the drone and get some over-head property shots and atmospheric, three-hundred-and-sixty-degree-view footage?" Dev made a circling motion with his finger. "Oh, and some panning, close-up clips. Like of the stair railings and the ornate windows, etcetera."

"Yeah, bro. We got you," Aaron said and chugged back what looked to be half of his energy drink. I felt jittery just watching him.

"We should probably do some dummy footage today, too, so we don't have to worry about it later."

I looked at Dev. "What's all that?"

He glanced over and smiled. "I forget you don't know this stuff. We can't get everything we need to edit a proper show from just the three days we are actively investigating. In order for the show to flow like it should to a viewer, there needs to be shots of the house and the grounds and us walking through the place and having discussions about the equipment we're using, etcetera. If we did all of that while actively investigating, we would bog it all down and likely never get any results, and if we didn't do any of that in-between stuff, it would be super stilted to someone viewing it second-hand. So, we shoot that stuff ahead of time and then have our people use it where needed in the editing process, so it all flows smoothly."

"That actually makes a lot of sense," I said, and he smiled and grabbed my hand, rubbing his thumb over my knuckles. When I looked back at the screen, I saw that everybody on there had the same look on their faces. Seemed the cat was out of the bag.

"Well, well, well," Paxton said.

"Good on you," Schuyler added.

Larken nodded with a huge smile on her face and raised her hands, both her thumbs up.

"Okay, guys, get it out of your systems. Yes, Hanlen and I are seeing each other. Sort of. It's new. Don't make a big deal about it," Dev said, shaking his head. I felt the blush rise on my neck to my cheeks and had to look away.

"I think I can safely speak for all of us when I say that we're thrilled," Larken said. "It's been a long time since I've seen you truly happy, Dev."

"Thanks, Lark," Dev said and then surprised me by leaning over and kissing my cheek. It stunned me enough that I looked up. The huge grins on everybody's faces lightened the weight of embarrassment in my chest but I still needed to refocus the attention.

"What do you need me to do?" I asked Dev and looked into his gorgeous aqua eyes.

He gave me that amazing grin of his. "Just be with me today. If you're okay with it, I might use you for some of the footage. You are the owner, after all. We don't always include the property owners outside of the initial filmed and staged interview, but sometimes it's necessary. In this case, since you guys didn't come to us for help, it wouldn't be absolutely necessary, but I think it'd be good. Thoughts?"

I mulled that over for a minute. "Yeah, I guess I could do that. But do you really want my disbelief on camera?"

He threw an arm around my shoulders and pulled me in for a squeeze. "We love a good skeptic."

When I looked up again, I saw that Schuyler was raising and waving her hand on screen while nodding. It made me laugh.

"Okay, I think we know what we have to do. Let me know if you need anything. Hanlen and I will meet those of you who are headed out there later. We're going to stop in and see Bea quick,"—he looked at me, and I nodded—"and then we'll come and find James for those filler reels."

Everybody murmured their agreements and disconnected. Once we were alone, I noticed Dev acting strangely again. Similar to how he'd been the night after we found Dustin, and this morning when he had to make his phone call.

"Hey," I said, grabbing his arm as he walked past me. "What's going on?"

He sighed and rubbed a hand through his silky curls. "You're very tuned in to me. It's great, but . . . maybe we should have a chat."

"Those words with that look on your face don't inspire much confidence. You may not have said, 'We need to talk,' but that's the gist."

He shook his head and tipped my chin up with a knuckle. "We *do* need to talk, but it's not anything bad."

"I'm not sure I believe you." He leaned in and placed a gentle kiss to my lips, lingering for a minute and letting our breaths mingle. I felt the electric charge I always did with Dev, and it made my breath catch.

"Come on," he said and grabbed my hand. "Let's delay our drive for a minute and head back upstairs where it's more comfortable."

"Okay," I answered and let him lead me back to his apartment. When we were seated comfortably on the couch with cups of coffee, Dev seemed to try to collect himself.

"So, I know you don't believe in any of this. But I really need you to try to have an open mind when I explain a few things to you. Can you do that?"

I honestly wasn't sure. While hanging out with

Dev and the cast and crew in the time I'd been here had made me question a few things and open my beliefs to a couple of others, I still wasn't a true believer. However, I was willing to try for Dev. "Yeah, I can do that."

I saw the relief pass through him. He physically relaxed and settled into the couch more, facing me. "As I mentioned before, all of us have different specialties and backgrounds. Larken is a natural-born witch. While I don't know her whole history, seeing as she's pretty tight-lipped about it, and I know it makes her uncomfortable when I pry, you've seen some of the things that she can do when we were setting up. Even to you, they had to be pretty impressive."

"They absolutely were. And you, too. I haven't seen you in action but there are definitely some unexplained things."

"Exactly," he said. "Given my lineage, it will probably come as no surprise to you that I am a Vodou priest. A Houngan. None of that is super important for what I wanted to talk to you about, but it will make some of the things you'll see during this investigation make more sense. Like the discussion I had with Lark earlier about casting a circle and me opening a way. Anyway, not important right now. If you have questions later, I'd love to talk to you about it."

I smiled but knew not to say anything. He seemed to need to get this out.

"Lark and I have different abilities when it comes to the departed. She's a psychic medium and can sense and hear them and get impressions of people, places, and things, but she can't see spirits beyond mists and shadow figures. I am sensitive to some of the things that she is, but I can summon ghosts and spirits and see and talk to them like I can see and chat with you sitting here."

I wasn't sure what to say. This was all beyond my comprehension and experiences. Yet a small part of me wanted to grab him and demand that he reach Reagan. That he get her to tell him what happened to her. For now, all I did was nod.

"But there's a catch," he continued.

"What's that?" I asked.

"They have to *want* to be seen. However, when they do, it's almost like having a child with no boundaries. They refuse to be ignored. You asked me what was wrong a few times now. Nothing's *wrong*. It's just that I've had some visitors and wasn't sure how to handle it with you around without scaring you off."

"Oh," I said. That actually made sense, and it made me feel a little warm inside. He respected my beliefs enough to not want to scare me away.

"The lovebirds I talked about earlier?"

"Yeah," I answered.

"It's my sister, Wren, and her guy, Findley."

I gasped. I couldn't help it. "You see your sister?"

"All the time," he said. "They're actually an integral part of the show. But they've also been trying to find Wren's killer. And you were right before when you said that you sensed that I'd lost someone else. We lost our cousin, Gunnie, some time ago. There were differences in the way that she was killed, but both Wren and I believe it may have been the same person. Maybe even one of their first kills."

I felt my heart drop. God, poor Dev. "I'm so sorry," I said, reaching out to touch his knee. He pulled me in, and I snuggled against him, lending him some strength. I knew if it were me, I would have an easier time talking if I didn't have to look someone in the eye anyway.

"Yeah. I know you can relate to that pain. The agony of not knowing. Of never getting anywhere. Not a day goes by where I don't think of them. That something doesn't remind me of the good times. All the times they made me smile. The stupid things we did together." He smiled, the expression a bit sad yet wistful.

"Anyway, the reason I've been so weird is that Wren and Findley have been coming to me pretty regularly lately with updates on the things that I sent them out to find but also because my cousin has been reaching out to people that aren't me, and I don't understand why. She's always been a little shy, even in life, more so in death—something I always loved about her, the contradiction of her endless collection of corsets and her much more demure personality.

But Lark said she contacted her, and then Wren told me this morning that she came to them, too. I don't know what's going on, but I don't want to pretend with you anymore or act strangely when around you because I'm trying to hide something that is as natural as breathing to me. Anyway, Wren asked me this morning if I thought you'd be open to something."

"What's that?" I asked.

"I can do a spell that will allow you to see them temporarily. They'd really like to meet you."

I pulled away and wrung my hands. "I don't know, Dev. You've opened my eyes to a lot, and I have to say that some things have definitely changed, but I'm not sure I'm ready for that. It's all still a bit fantastical to me, though I do know that there are unexplained things beyond my comprehension for sure."

He smiled. "That's exactly what I told her. We don't have to, but I wanted you to know, and I wanted you to have the choice."

"I appreciate that," I said and then leaned in to give him a kiss. "Was that all?"

"Yeah, that's all. For now." He kissed me again. "What do you say we hit the road?"

"Absolutely. Let's go see Bea."

Chapter 17

Dev

I watched myself on screen over Lennie's head. "*Here, about thirty minutes outside of N'awlins, we will set up shop for seventy-two hours to get to the bottom of the mysteries of Arborwood. A two-hundred-and-fifty-year-old ancestral planta- tion home rife with history and teeming with spirits. A place I've wanted to explore since the show first aired. It is our duty to give the dead a voice, to bring light to the departed oppressed, and to bring answers to the living. It is our calling. Our passion. This . . . is* Haunted New Orleans."

"Yeah, that looks great." I looked over at Hanlen. "What do you think?"

She scrunched up her face and nodded. "I like it. A lot. It's fabulous. The camera work is amazing with you sitting on the stool on the driveway like that, and the house in the background slightly out of focus."

I stole a quick kiss and then looked around at who remained. "I think we're good here for today. Everything's set, and we got some great footage. That random fog that rolled in after that quick shower was perfect."

"Right?" Aaron said as he strolled up, taking his last bite of whatever he'd grabbed for a snack. The guy was always eating or drinking something. Though I supposed with his body-builder physique, he burned calories faster than the rest of us. "I don't think we could have asked for better filler footage than we got today. And this one,"—he hitched a thumb at Hanlen —"was made for television. The camera loves you."

I looked over and saw Hanlen blush and smiled. "He's right, you know? You saw how well those scenes went when we watched them back."

"That's only because I had great interviewers who made me feel comfortable."

"Nah, it's all you." I tucked that wayward wave behind her ear and ran my fingers across her jaw on the retreat. I couldn't seem to stop touching her, and was grateful that she appeared to not only tolerate it outside of closed doors but also enjoy it.

"Lark?" I called. She looked my way from her spot in the corner where I knew she was placing some selenite. I'd asked her to put shards in the four cardinal corners of the house to help with protection but also to ramp up the energy. Normally, we'd use quartz or amethyst as an amplifier, but for some reason, my instincts had told me to use selenite this time because of its ability to keep light and energy flowing and allow messages from higher forces to come through. Lark had wholeheartedly agreed.

"Yeah?" she answered.

"Are you good? Do you need anything from me before we head out? I want to go check on Burke. We still haven't heard anything from him, and I'm starting to worry. I need the data he gathered on the woman Harper believes is Chloe Aillet, given the research she did after interviewing the Whitakers. And I just want to make sure he's all right."

She smiled and waved a hand, still full of selenite shards. "No, go on. I'm good. Just have a few things to finish up here and we'll be ready to go tomorrow. What time do you want us here?"

"Um, let me send a group text later. I have to do some thinking about how to attack the next few days. As we know, the things we uncover will dictate a lot of it, but I'm not sure how early I want to start. We should all get as much rest as we can since we'll be going overnight for the next couple of days, at least."

"Sounds good," she answered. "Drive safely."

I grabbed Hanlen's hand and started to walk away when I heard Lark call out. "Oh, wait. Dev?"

I turned, and Hanlen turned with me. "Yeah?"

"Um . . ." She cocked her head for a minute and

stared off into space. "Whew, that was a rush. Okay, ah . . . I have no idea what this means, but you need to look to the water and beware of false prophets. Or maybe . . . false idols? I don't know."

My stomach tumbled. "Message from spirit?" I asked.

"No," she answered. "Just a psychic flash. And as you know, they don't always make sense in the moment."

"But they're always right. At least, *you* are. Thanks for the heads-up, Lark."

"Take care, you guys," she said and went back to her task.

I retook Hanlen's hand and walked through the courtyard to the front lawn. Squeezing her fingers, I asked, "Did that freak you out?"

"Actually, no," she said. "I still don't get it, and I'm not sure how I feel about it all, but I've seen enough in the time that I've been here to know that not all things need to be explained. Some things just are."

"Well, well, well. Is cynical Hanlen Arbor becoming a believer?" I turned her to me and wrapped her in my arms, staring down at her. She smiled up at me.

"I didn't say that. But I do have a lot more respect for what you guys do."

"I'll take it," I said and then took her lips in a passionate kiss. She melted into me and gave as good as she got. When we came up for air, both of us were breathing heavily.

"It is really too bad that I have some things to take care of because I would love nothing more than to take you to bed and ravish you until the sun comes up."

She squeezed my butt. "I thought you said we needed sleep."

"Oh, we do. But we can nap between rounds. And I fully plan on taking advantage of the morning hours we don't have to be here to sleep with you in my arms."

"Such a charmer," she said and then kissed me quickly again before climbing behind the wheel of her SUV.

When I was buckled into the passenger seat, she turned to me. "Where to?" she asked.

"I really want to go and check on Burke. He lives in Bucktown on Lake Ponchartrain."

"Do you have his address on you, or do we need to go into the city first?" She looked over at me as she navigated the drive to the main road.

"I've got it." I held up my cell. "Just head that way, and I'll direct you once we get closer."

"Sounds good."

Not too long later, we pulled up to a house on the 17th Street Canal, fishing boats heading out onto the lake beyond the property. A columned porch encircled the entire whitewashed dwelling, the setting sun creating a perfect backdrop.

"Wow," Hanlen said as she put the SUV in park. "Nice place. What does Burke do again? Or what did he do before he started working for you?"

"He's an associate professor and a local historian. He also dabbles in some web sleuth stuff. There are all sorts of true crime aficionados out there that lend their support for cold cases and such. But I think his family has money from generations of being in the seafood industry."

"Ah, that makes sense," she said and unbuckled her belt. "It looks pretty quiet here. I don't see many lights on in the house. There's a dim glow in the corner window over there, but I don't see anything else. And, strangely, my investigator instincts are buzzing. Maybe it's just because nobody's heard from him, but I'm glad we came."

"Yeah, me, too," I said and got out of the SUV. I checked my phone again, just to make sure that Burke hadn't texted or called me back. When I saw no new notifications, I stuffed it away and waited for Hanlen to join me at the front of the SUV. "Ready?" I asked.

"Yep, let's do this. I have a really bad feeling for some reason and want to make sure that he's okay."

I couldn't agree more. The minute I stepped foot on Burke's land, my instincts started screaming.

We walked up the porch steps and rang the bell. When I didn't hear anything from inside, I knocked.

Hanlen stood beside me, taking in her surroundings. I could almost see the gears in her mind working. We'd talked about her job, and I could see why she was so good at it. She had innate ability, both natural and supernatural.

I knocked one more time without an answer. Just as I was about to give up and tell Hanlen that we should go, I saw Burke walk around the side of the house from his backyard, his form backlit by the setting sun, creating a silhouette in the dusk.

"Hey, man," I called. "Everything okay? Where have you been? We've been worried sick."

Hanlen looked where my attention was focused and then turned to me. "Dev, who are you talking to?"

My heart sank, and my breath caught in my lungs.

Well, fuck.

Chapter 18

Hanlen

"Dev? What's going on?" I asked, my instincts immediately picking up on the shift in Dev's body language.

He looked at me and blew a breath out through
his lips before biting his bottom one. "I just saw
Burke."

Confused, I looked around, not seeing anybody.
"Where? Did he walk into the back?"

Dev shook his head and then looked to the sky as
if searching for answers. Or strength. "He's actually
right there and coming closer." He pointed.

I looked where he indicated but still saw nothing.
"I don't see him. Is he behind the gazebo?"

Dev scrubbed his hands over his face. "No, he's

right there. But you can't see him. Fuck, Hanlen. That's Burke's spirit. Something happened to him. He's not with us anymore. He's on the other side of the veil."

Burke's . . . spirit. I was instantly nauseated. "Are you messing with me?"

Before I even finished my sentence, he turned me to face him and shook his head adamantly. "No. I would never do that. When you told me that you didn't know who I was talking to, it all clicked. Remember, I told you, to me, if a ghost wants to be seen, they look and sound just like you and me. The only difference is, I can't touch them. I really thought that was Burke—alive-and-well Burke—not his spirit. We need to go and see what happened. Sometimes, ghosts linger or return to the place they felt the safest, but I have a feeling that he's here to talk to me. I don't want him to stick around longer than he has to if that's not what he wants. Are you going to be okay with this? It'll probably be really weird for you to only hear one side of the conversation."

"I'll be fine as long as you relay what you learn. Right now, I'm in investigator mode. I need to know what happened more than I'm worried about how we'll get that information."

"Good answer," he said and kissed my temple before walking in the direction of the side of the house. As we got nearer, I felt the hairs on my arms and neck stand at attention. It had to be my imagination. Still, I tried not to let it make me uneasy, especially since I had the advantage that most people didn't have and knew why it was happening.

"Hey, man," Dev said, and my stomach tumbled again. The vivacious, funny guy that I'd spent time with at Lafitte's was no longer with us. Why was life so unfair, taking those who were so very alive well before their time? Those thoughts made me think of Reagan again, and I had to take some deep breaths and clear my head so I wouldn't get mired in the sorrow and not pay attention to what Dev was saying.

"I'm going to paraphrase what you tell me so that I don't leave Hanlen in the lurch, okay?" He actually smiled, and I wondered what Burke had said. "Yeah, we're together," he said, letting me guess what Burke had questioned. "Thanks, man."

Dev led me up onto Burke's porch again and indicated for me to take a seat on the swing. I did, and he sat next to me, still looking at the steps. "What happened?" he asked the air.

After a minute, he turned to me. "He said he doesn't really know. Apparently, he came home from the historical society and was ambushed in the garage. He said he knows that something bad happened to him, gets flashes of some pretty horrific things, but he can't actually remember it." He took a breath. "That's not uncommon for tragic deaths. Wren didn't remember her murder either. Didn't even know she was dead until Findley told her. It may come to Burke eventually, and it may not. Sometimes, it's the universe's way of wiping the slate clean so they can make a proper decision how to handle their afterlife."

God, I felt so bad for Burke. He was probably about my age, like Dev was and Wren would have been. I couldn't imagine having my life cut short like that. Or even younger, like Reagan's had been. And he had been so excited to be working with Dev on the show. It really seemed like he'd found his niche. God, it was so horrible. So terribly unfair.

Dev had tuned back into something Burke was saying, and I waited patiently. "He said that he woke up down by the lake." Which made me think of what Lark said to him before we'd left Arborwood.

"Look to the water," I said, remembering. "Well, it seems we likely know what she was referring to, at least with that part. How do you want to handle this? You have a seasoned investigator with you, but we are also dealing with the third death surrounding us in a very short time. You and I both know that we had nothing to do with any of them, but Watkins and Miller may not feel the same. Do you think we should call this in now? Do they know what you can do?" God, I couldn't believe I was even asking that. Did *I* know what he could do? Did I believe now? I searched deep and realized that, yes, I thought I did. My, my, how the times had changed. The subtle changes in me over the course of this trip, mostly attributed to the man now at my side, had cultivated a profound shift within me. I'd have to examine that closer later, but for now, I would take comfort in the fact that I wasn't freaking out about it. There was too much else going on.

"Let's go take a look, and then we'll call. I think it's important for us to see things before we report it." He paused. "Burke agrees. Okay, let's head down there and see if we can find anything."

"Lead the way," I said and stood.

When we got to the back of the house, I saw that Burke had a floating dock and a tiny personal beach. At first cursory glance, nothing appeared out of the ordinary, but as we got closer, my hackles rose more. It was the only way I could describe the feeling that swept over me. I could tell that Dev felt the same. His body tightened, and the grip he had on my hand became slippery from the sweat that now dotted his palm. After another perusal from left to right, my gaze snagged on something sticking out from behind a big boulder down by the dock, at the line where the grass met the sand and rocks. I pointed.

"Down there," I said, and Dev's gaze followed my finger. He nodded and picked up the pace, walking towards whatever it was I had seen. We were running out of light. Burke had some post lights down here, but it was still dark. I let go of Dev's hand and pulled out my cell, turning on the flashlight app. He nodded and did the same with his. When we got closer, I saw that what I'd caught sight of were boots. Nice ones that disappeared into dark denim. Oh, God.

"Fuck," Dev said aloud, echoing my thoughts. I had a feeling I knew exactly what we'd find when we got down there, and I wasn't sure I could handle it. I hadn't seen August's body, but Bea had told us exactly what she'd found and how she'd found him. While I'd seen Dustin Reynolds' corpse, I didn't have a personal connection to the man. Between those and what I knew would soon fill my vision, I wanted to vomit because all I could think about was Reagan's drained form. I stopped in my tracks.

"Hey," Dev said, backtracking a bit and making me look at him. "Are you okay? I know this can't be easy."

"No, I'm not okay. But I can do this. Just give me a second."

He pulled me into his body and held me close, his oak moss scent enveloping me and calming something inside me. I took a few deep breaths and then stepped away, ready to see this through.

"Let's do this."

We walked the rest of the way to the rock and rounded the side of it. The sight before me knocked out every breath I had left and staggered me. I actually took a step back, my hand flying to my mouth, my eyes rounding.

"Holy fuck," Dev said. I couldn't agree more. While Reynolds' body had been gruesome with its slashed throat, and disturbing in how it had been arranged, this was like something out of a nightmare —or a horror movie. Burke was posed in nature, the same as Dustin and August had been—at least according to Detective Miller—but this was something else. More heinous. More depraved. More . . . personal, somehow. He lay prone with his hands crossed over his middle, his legs straight out, that damn token or coin on his forehead like the others. But where the others looked almost peaceful in death despite the bloodless wounds, Burke was a mess. There was no other way to describe it.

His skin had that unnatural waxy pallor that the others had, likely a result of the exsanguination, and a little bit of the elements I supposed. But nearly every inch of Burke's skin bore a gash. It was like death by a thousand cuts. And his eyes . . . oh, God, his eyes. They had been removed. Almost surgically, the gaping holes like hell pits. He, too, had a slit throat, but while Dustin's had been almost surgical in its cleanliness, this was ragged and raw, as if the monster who had done this had used the dullest implement possible to inflict the most pain. There were other pieces of flesh missing from his body, as well, almost as if someone had torn chunks free. Maybe even with teeth.

Jesus.

"This is different," Dev said.

"It is. Definitely more rage filled. Something's happening to our killer. Something . . . I don't know.

Set them off? Not only have the kills been much closer together—at least from what I've gathered about the cases—but they're escalating. And yet becoming sloppier. All I can hope is that the scene is sloppy, too. This sicko needs to be caught." I looked up to see Dev staring at a spot just beyond the body, tears in his eyes.

"I'm so damn sorry, man. So sorry. You didn't deserve this. And I hate that you have to see it." He wiped his nose and nodded, presumably at something Burke said.

"I wish I knew, brother." He paused for a minute, looking as if he were listening. "You'll need to work through this earthly trauma. You can venture out, but you'll eventually have to return home to recharge since this is where you entered the veil. After that, if you want and are receptive, I would be honored to perform a ritual for you to help free your soul and allow you to enter a place of rest if that's what you want. But until then—and even after if you so decide to forego the ritual and are open to it—I'd love for you to help with the investigation at Arborwood. Maybe even work with some of my other departed family and friends to get to the bottom of this asshole wreaking havoc on our city." He nodded, and then a small, soft smile graced his face.

"I told you. I found you for a reason. We were meant to work together. This may not be what we had planned, but you are and will always be a part of the team. Until you decide you've had enough. I mean, why would I pass up access to the Akashic Records by a historian?" He smiled, and then laughed. "Truer words have never been spoken."

"What did he say?" I asked, not believing those words had actually come out of my mouth.

"He said that I would be stupid if I didn't jump at the chance to work with a researcher and historian who basically now knows everything."

"What are the Akashic Records?" I asked, needing a bit more to understand the context.

"For those who believe in divine wisdom," Dev said, "the Akashic Records are a compendium of all universal events. Thoughts, words, emotions, intent . . . everything that has ever occurred or *will* occur in terms of all life forms—both human and not."

"Geez. That's intense," I said.

"Yeah," Dev answered. "I know it's a lot to take in, but you have to admit, it's a comforting thought."

He wasn't wrong. If those we'd lost were wherever they ended up and inherently *knew* when things would happen and how they tied into events of the past, it would be like having the best guardians ever. Maybe Reagan *was* watching out for me and guiding me. I loved that thought, but it didn't stem the pain I still felt. And I had another question.

"But if they know everything that happened and will happen, then why don't we already know who killed them?"

"Unfortunately, that's not how it works. I mean, it is," he said, "but there are rules. One of the biggest ones being that they cannot know their own fates—past, present, or future—and they can only access the records if they actively go searching. It isn't like just having the entire knowledge of the universe instantly in their heads. They can easily access things to get answers, but not if it pertains to them. There has to be balance. And because people like me exist and can talk to those who have access to that knowledge, someone, somewhere, decided that it wouldn't be fair. Not to mention, as we've found, if the person being researched has ties to someone who has ties and so forth, the knowledge gets . . . muddy and a bit obscured. Which is why my sister and Findley have yet to discover who killed Wren, even though they've had other murders to investigate."

"Well, that's bullshit," I said, and Dev laughed.

"You're not wrong," he agreed.

Dev said goodbye to the historian, telling him that he didn't think it would be a good idea for Burke to stick around when the police came to handle things with his body, and I absolutely had to agree. He'd been through enough. I couldn't believe I was entertaining the idea that a psychic and a ghost had just led us to a murdered corpse, but I couldn't deny the facts. And I couldn't ignore that I felt compelled to believe just about every word that came out of Dev's mouth. It was unusual yet comforting.

"I suppose we should call this in," Dev said, and I nodded. He made the call, ringing Detective Miller directly, which I thought was a great idea, and then we waited. I was sure that this would be a long-ass night. Again. So much for us getting some rest and some private time before the shoot.

How in the world had a trip to New Orleans to oversee a frickin' TV show turned into such a cluster-fuck of murder and mayhem?

Chapter 19

Dev

We'd gotten maybe three hours of sleep. Detective Watkins had been determined in trying to find a way to make us look guilty, while a frustrated and exhausted Detective Miller tried to get to the bottom of the real story. Between once again spending hours at the police station, us checking Hanlen out of her hotel, and simply not being able to shut off our minds, it had been a restless night. After Hanlen had shared some information about the dreams she'd been having, I'd realized that a dark spirit had likely been visiting her. We'd moved her things to my place immediately.

I'd texted everybody on the show to let them know

what'd happened and assumed that those who saw it didn't get much sleep either. This case would be a rough one for all of us. It was maybe the first time in forever that I sort of wished we didn't find much on the first night, which would allow us to beg off a bit early and start again tomorrow. The only possible positive was that if history were any indication, the more vulnerable you were during an investigation, the more contact could be established if the spirits decided to be cooperative, so this *could* be a boon—as horrible as it was to think that.

Hanlen walked up the stairs with Myst after taking her outside, and I set aside my tablet. "Hey, you two."

"Hey, yourself," Hanlen said with a jaw-cracking yawn. "It's after noon, and yet I feel like it's dawn." She yawned again. "Geez," she said with a head shake. "Sorry. There is quite possibly not enough caffeine in the world for this day."

I stretched, my neck and back popping in the silence of the room. "You aren't kidding."

Myst went to curl up in her bed, and Hanlen ran a hand through her long hair.

"Come here," I said and wiggled my fingers at her. She rolled her neck and shuffled over, plopping down on the couch and then lying across my lap. I massaged her scalp and raked my fingers through her silky strands. She let out a little hum of appreciation.

"Mmm, that feels nice." She sighed, and I smiled. It did feel nice. Despite everything, all of this felt nice.

The joy of being with Hanlen wasn't something I had expected, but I'd known there was something between us from the moment I ran into her on the street. And that sense of rightness had only increased as the days passed in her company. Our relationship had been one forged in the fires of tragedy and sorrow, but there was no denying that I was falling hard for Hanlen Arbor.

"Are you ready for today?" I asked.

"Besides wanting to fall asleep on my feet already . . . yeah, actually. I am." She smiled up at me, and I brushed my fingers across her cheek. She shifted, and her necklace slipped free of her pajama top. I looked at the golden veve, the sigil sparking in the light and with the magic imbued in it and wondered once again why it was extra-familiar to me.

I knew the symbol well. I had a similar talisman on my keychain for my patron lwa. But there was something else familiar about it. Something that resonated with me and my energy and magic. Still, the why behind that remained elusive. I knew if I let myself keep it on the periphery, my intuition would eventually fill in the holes, but my curiosity got the better of me.

I fingered the gold and picked up the pendant, rubbing it between my fingers and feeling a jolt. Interesting. There was more than just residual protection magic in the talisman. There was soul magick.

Someone had literally put a bit of themselves into this piece of jewelry.

"Who gave you this again?" I asked.

"The best friend I told you I lost? My sister for all intents and purposes? The one who was murdered? This was hers. She never took it off. We basically grew up together, at least during our later teen years, and then we moved in together in the city after gradua-tion." She shifted to stare up at me, and the look of sorrow in her eyes nearly made tears spring to mine.

"The morning after the police notified me of what'd happened, I found this in a bowl on the hallway table. To this day, I still don't know why she wasn't wearing it that night. Like I said, she never took it off. But it was there, and now *I've* rarely taken it off."

I let the veve drop to her chest and gently pinched her chin, leaning down to kiss her sweetly. "I'm so sorry, *mon amour*." The natural use of the endearment startled me for a second but then settled like a warm weight in my chest. I did love her.

I loved Hanlen.

Whoa.

I brushed the hair back from her face. "What was her name?" I asked.

A dreamy smile filled her expression. "Her name was Reagan, and she was the most incredible human being on the face of the planet. Reagan Legendre."

Everything in me locked. My muscles, the blood rushing through my veins, the breath in my lungs.

Merde.

Reagan Legendre. Daughter of Jacques and Phillipa. The second marriage between those two distantly related families in history, the first being Marie Laveau's youngest daughter, Marie Philomene to Emile Alexandre Legendre.

Whose many-times great-granddaughter became Reagan Legendre.

My cousin.

Better known to me as *Gunnie*.

Holy shit!

"Hey, what's wrong?" Hanlen asked, placing her soft palm on my cheek and bringing me back to the present. "Are you seeing something?"

"Message from spirit," I lied. How in the world did I tell her that her murdered best friend was *my* murdered cousin without bringing up all sorts of hurt? I decided it could wait until later. Nothing about this was pressing at the moment.

"So," I said, "are you ready to get up and get set for a long-ass day and night?"

She sat and stretched. "I am. Make me another cup of coffee while I hop in the shower?"

"Absolutely," I said and grasped her cheek and neck, bringing her in for a thorough kiss, moving down to swirl my tongue over the pulse point in her neck and then moving up to nibble on her earlobe.

"Mmm," she said. "If you keep doing that, I'm going to say screw the show and keep you in bed all day."

I nipped her again and then moved to place another kiss to her delectable lips. "I would like nothing more. But . . . as they say, the show must go on." I rose, bringing her with me, a small squeak escaping her lips. When I let her back to her feet, I made sure to let her body slide down mine so she could feel how much I wished that answer was different.

"Deveraux Glapion, you tease."

"Guilty as charged," I said and kissed her again before swatting her bitable ass. "Off with you. I need to make my goddess some coffee."

"Goddess, huh? I like it. I think I could get used to that." She raised a brow with a quirk of her lips and then sauntered off to the bathroom, an extra sway in her hips. Just as she was about to disappear into the room, she looked over her shoulder, threw me a sassy wink, blew me a kiss, and then disappeared.

I groaned and shook my head.

She might be the death of me.

———

THE PLANTATION LOOKED amazing in the mid-afternoon light, the live oaks casting shadows on the façade and creeping across the ground like searching hands. I'd asked Aaron and James to get some additional shots of the place because it looked so good right now. Almost as if she were dressing up for the party to come.

The gang was gathered a bit down the driveway where Larken had set her circle the other day. I'd just gotten off the phone with Remy, and he'd walked me through what he'd done to get things ready. I was grateful that he'd come out here while he wasn't feeling well, but because he was still sick, we would be without our best tech.

To add insult to injury, Van had called about a family emergency, something with their grandmother up north, so we were navigating the first shooting day without my two engineers, too. I'd called in another temp that we used from time to time, Jeremy. I didn't know him all that well and thought he was a little odd, truth be told. He was super quiet and seemed to look *through* people at times, and there was always a hint of that warning energy I got when people weren't all the way on the side of good, but he was a hard worker and, sometimes, beggars couldn't be choosy. Which was where I stood now. I needed the help, he was available, and he was ready to do the job. I just hoped that nothing went wrong that needed to be fixed immediately, and that Remy and the super twins would be back to work soon. I was spoiled. My team was the best, and I hated to be without even one of them.

I looked back at Lark. The witch stood near the salt and dirt line, her long, black duster sweater blowing in the breeze, the pentagram necklace at her throat winking in the light. She'd smudged us all with sage earlier and gave us each a unique, charged and blessed crystal to carry with us in our pockets.

She raised her blade high overhead and then turned to each of the four cardinal directions, her lips moving with her invocation.

Hanlen leaned in to me to whisper, "What's with the dagger?"

"It's called an athame. It's a ceremonial tool that she uses to direct energy. Have you ever seen the *Harry Potter* movies?" I asked, and she nodded. "You know how they use their wands? It's the same concept, albeit greatly simplified."

She nodded and backed away a bit, rubbing her arms. She was most definitely sensitive if she could feel the energy that Lark was currently raising.

Lark made an upward slicing motion in front of her, ground to sky, and then said, "From north to east and south to west, hale to the guardians. I, Larken, sister, daughter, friend, enter this circle with perfect love and perfect trust, for the good of all, according to free will, so mote it be." She stepped across the salt and graveyard dirt line and then turned to face us.

"Now, each of you. Step across the line and say, 'I enter this circle with perfect love and perfect trust.'"

She looked at Hanlen. "I know this is new and probably really weird to you. Are you okay?"

Hanlen glanced at me and then back to Lark. "Yeah, I'm good," she said. "Actually, I'll go first." She smiled. "I enter this circle with perfect love and perfect trust." She stepped over the line and went to stand behind Lark.

I was so proud of her. I knew she still had some reservations, but she was taking to this bright new world with surprising aplomb.

We each followed suit, entering the sacred space that Lark had created.

"I ask the Lord and Lady to bless this circle so that we may be free and protected within this space." She ran her athame down the same line she'd drawn up earlier. "The circle is now cast, sacred space is made, and all within its boundaries, both living and not, are under the protection of the maiden, mother, and crone until the circle is closed. So mote it be."

When I knew the cameras weren't on us, I turned off my microphone and pulled Hanlen to me to kiss the top of her head. "Are you ready? Now you get to see *me* in action." I smiled, and she grinned up at me.

"Abso-frickin-lutely," she said.

We all walked to the courtyard entryway, and everybody took up the places we'd discussed earlier, Aaron and James on their marks and ready to record the different angles we needed. I turned to James.

"We're ready to enter this amazing two-hundred-

and-fifty-year-old plantation home and see what awaits us. This dwelling is rich with history and rife with stories. Something our crewmember, Burke Mathers, would have loved. Burke passed suddenly before the filming of this episode. On behalf of myself and the entire cast and crew of *Haunted New Orleans*, I want to dedicate this episode to him." I turned to Aaron so they'd get a different angle for editing. "This one's for you, brother. Thank you for everything."

I walked to the side of the entryway wall and knocked three times. "Knocking is a ritual gesture." I turned to the camera briefly. "It is also a sign of respect to let anyone inside know that we're coming."

I moved to the middle of the space and knelt, taking the things I needed from my mesh bag. Everybody closed in around me, and I felt Hanlen's soft palm on my shoulder for a brief moment before she backed away to join the others. It gave me strength.

"The Guardian of the Crossroads has a personal symbol. A geometric design known as a veve. All of the lwas have one, each special to them." I started drawing the sigil. "Papa Legba, dealer of destinies, intermediary to the spirit world." I finished the veve and sat back on my heels for a moment, gathering my energy.

I placed my palm over the middle of the veve and whistled. "To all the spirits of all directions . . . We call upon you spirits of fire, I want you to come through." I lit the candle sitting at the south point of the sigil.

"The spirits of water, we request you." I sprinkled Florida water in a circle around the veve, starting on the west side, the blessed cologne acting like holy water and as a connection to the element.

"The spirits of air, we request you." I waved a feather over the symbol, starting in the east.

"The spirits of earth, we call to you." I reached into a small pouch and sprinkled some graveyard dirt mixed with tobacco on the sigil, starting in the north, the earthy herb mixture representing the element and also acting as an offering to the lwas.

"We give offerings, as well, to feed your way," I sprinkled some peanuts over the veve, one of Papa Legba's favorites, and then took a drink from my flask, spraying spiced rum in three directions—also a favorite of not only the Guardian of the Crossroads but also other spirits. "Does anyone have any coins?" I asked.

As we'd discussed, Hanlen, Larken, and Schuyler came forward with coins, dropping them onto the sigil.

"I, Dev Glapion, descendant of Marie Laveau. I, Devereaux, of many names in the past and in the future, call upon the spirits of this place and to Papa Legba. We ask that we may communicate with you. May we see you, may we hear you, may we photograph you with

great respect. Open the way. May I present my friends."
I turned to the group. "Please state your full names."
They each did as requested. "We call upon them. We let
you open the way for them to come through today." I
whistled again and smacked my palm left, up, right, and
in the middle three times. "Open the way."

I stood and turned to face the group, smiling.
"The way is now open." I tucked my things into my
bag and walked into the courtyard backwards, turning
to the camera once I was in shadow. "Things in
Vodou and Voodoo are mirror images. Therefore, it's
always more powerful to walk through a portal backwards." The group followed suit, and once we were all
inside, I motioned for the camera guys to cut for a
second.

I walked to Hanlen. "Are you okay?" I asked. She
looked up at me, her expression a little awed.

"I'm . . . I'm great. That was amazing. I'm still so
new to all of this, especially believing in any of it, but
there's no denying the way the things that you and
Larken do make me feel. Can I kiss you, or would that
be breaking some rule?"

I laughed and wrapped my hand around the nape
of her neck, tipping her head back with gentle pressure on her chin with my thumb so I could take her
lips. "You can kiss me anytime you want. The lwas
love it—they're all quite randy. And so do I."

She placed another quick peck to my cheek and

stepped away, spinning in a circle to take in the court-yard. "Where are we starting?" she asked.

I gestured for the guys to start recording again, and the whole crew did a walk-through of the house on all levels, doing some quick EVP recording sessions and checking for electromagnetic energy with the K2 meters. We got some voice responses in the master bedroom, the kitchen, and in the old cold storage space off the dining room. Larken got some pretty strong impressions on the widow's walk, so I told her to set up her Handycam and stay up there to do some automatic-writing work, where she let the spirits use her as a conduit to communicate by scribbling on a notepad. She could hear them, and so could the recorder if they so desired, but sometimes she got great results doing it this way, and it stopped her from being inundated with excessive voices and flashes.

Padre and Sky took the cold storage room since both Lark and I had felt the energy in there was a bit more malignant, and I figured it wouldn't hurt to have a skeptic and an ex-priest dealing with that. I sent Dakota into the kitchen so she could use her psychometry and read some of the objects in there, and Hanlen and I took the bedroom. Everybody else was in the command center in the corner of the courtyard, keeping watch on all the rooms and the property, observing, waiting, and listening.

"Why don't you take a seat on the bed?" I said to Hanlen while scanning the space with our thermal imaging camera. "The device I have here," I said, "records the temperature of objects in the room. If a temperature variance happens, it will show up on the display and record the anomaly. Spirits most often present themselves as cold energy, which renders as shades of blue, so anything that differs from the quote-unquote normal, will show up here."

I took a seat on a chair near the bed and turned on the voice recorder, setting it on the edge of the night table. "Is there anybody here who would like to communicate with us?" I asked, sweeping the camera over the room. "We don't mean any disrespect. We'd just like to know who you are and why you remain." I paused. "Can you tell us your name? If you talk really loudly into that red light there,"—I pointed at the recorder—"we will be able to hear you." I didn't usually let on during a show that I could see the departed. They didn't normally manifest like that to me anyway, especially if I had no connection to them. The only spirits I communicated with in any physical way during a show were the lwas and my family and friends, and that was generally done off-camera.

I glanced at Hanlen and saw her bring her knees up to her chest, wrapping her arms around them. "Is this your home?" I asked. "We heard you briefly earlier but weren't sure what you were trying to tell us. Can you repeat that?" I waited and then startled a bit when I heard Hanlen's voice.

"Are you an Arbor?" she asked. "Are you one of

Arborwood's workers? Are you watching over the property?"

I couldn't hold back the smile that overtook my face at her joining in on the investigation. "Okay, let's take a listen to this," I said and stopped the recording, backing up to the beginning of the session. We listened to the questions without any responses until Hanlen chimed in. Clear as day on the recording, we heard intelligent responses to her inquiries in a soft, feminine voice.

"Are you an Arbor?"

"YES."

The answers to the last two questions were no and yes respectively. I thought I knew who this might be. I started the recorder again.

"Myrtle Arbor," I said. "Is that you? . . . Are you still here to see to your kin?" I paused. "Why do you bother the renters while they're here? . . . They say they see a woman in white a lot in this room and the halls. Is that you?" Another pause. "Is there anything that you need us to do for you?"

"Do you really think this is my many-times-great-grandmother?" Hanlen asked.

"I do," I said. "From all the research we gathered, she died in the house. In this room, actually. It makes sense. And she was a fierce woman. Extremely protective of those under her care. It seems entirely plausible that she's our woman in white. That she'd remain to continue her matronly duties."

When we listened to the recording, I got one of the most compelling pieces of EVP evidence I'd ever received on an investigation. The recorder had still been running when Hanlen asked me her question about her ancestor. As if the person were standing right next to us, the recording revealed three words in that same soft, feminine voice.

"HAN - LEN. COME . . . HOME."

Chapter 20

"You'll be silent forever, and I'll be gone in the dark."
~Joseph James DeAngelo, Jr.

The darkness inside him reigned. Celebrated. The festivities of the other night had been euphoric, bringing not only vitality and completion but also a sense of accomplishment. His sacrifice had fought hard, infusing their donation with extra energy, making the act more sacred. Why hadn't he understood that before? The fear was like a delicious additive, an infusion of power, making the blood like hot chocolate . . . made more delicious by the screams.

He *would* experience it again. Now that he knew, he would never go back. He couldn't. Some things never changed, but this definitely would. As would his newfound glory of taking pieces of his sacrifice unto himself, above and beyond their font of life. He could still taste the smoky sweetness of the flesh as it slid down his throat, chased by the drink from his chalice of life-giving elixir.

He needed to be strong for her. Effervescent. Fate had unexpectedly brought her back into his life, and this time he would have her. There would be no getting away from him. No second chances for her, no second choices for him. But to have her, he had to make sure he was at his best. And that meant borrowing from those the darkness deemed worthy.

He didn't have anyone new in mind yet. But he would find the perfect specimen. He would uncover the one who would allow him to ascend and finally claim what was rightfully his.

He glanced at the picture he had secured to his truck visor, running his finger over the fine planes of her face, taking in her natural smile that he'd caught when she was unawares.

She was special. So very special. The one who would help him become what he was always meant to be. He wished he could see her in person right now. Take in her vitality, if only by being in her proximity. But that would have to wait. He had other things to attend to first. Things that would be important when he made his next move.

But he *would* see her again.

Soon.

Chapter 21

Hanlen

I couldn't believe how tired I was. Yet wired. The investigation had been a rush and a half. I could see the appeal. The adrenaline was unlike anything else, and the pride and excitement anytime anything turned up was like a hit of sunshine. An endorphin rush that was better than the best designer drug—or so I assumed. But we were wrapping things up now for the night, and I could feel the crash coming on.

"Hey, Dev?" I called.

"Yeah?" he said and came walking over.

"I think we should stay here tonight. Why drive all the way back into the city? That is, if you can get ahold of your neighbor to see to Myst."

He nodded. "That's actually a great idea. I'd like to do some investigating on the property tomorrow, and it would be better to do it early so we know what we're getting into when we hit dead time for day two."

He'd told me that *dead time* was what they called it when they went lights-out and began the investigation in earnest.

"You can let anyone else know that they're welcome to stay if they want, too. There are eight bedrooms in the place. And the carriage house is furnished also," I added.

"I need to tell them to wrap up for the night anyway. Unfortunately, the walkie is dead. The ghosts must have drained the energy." He grinned. "As for the carriage house, I'd rather not have anyone out there just yet since we haven't investigated it, but having everyone close and ready to go would be great. We can have anyone who heads back bring us some stuff from the city, but I'm ninety percent sure that most of us have extra clothes and things in our bags or vehicles. It's just something we learned to do on investigations because you never know what might happen, especially during the times you have to investigate in the elements."

He took out his cell and texted the group, presumably so he didn't have to walk all over and tell everyone in person, since everybody was spread out in the house and on the property. I thought about what I'd seen as we walked through the courtyard. I was pretty sure that every room was ready for guests. We generally always kept it that way because of the rentals, and I knew that Bea and the cleaning crew had just been here, and the agency knew to check things like soap and towels and whatnot.

Dev walked up to me and kissed my cheek. "Everybody but Dakota and our temp tech grip, Jeremy, are staying. They thought it was a great idea, too. And I was right, everybody had enough stuff to get by for the night."

I felt a weird sense of relief that Jeremy wasn't staying. The guy seemed good at his job, but he was a little strange. Somewhere around my age, maybe a little older, he seemed a bit of a loner and just had this weird . . . dead look in his eyes a lot of the time. It was an expression I'd seen often working with criminals. But who was I to judge? I didn't know his background, and even if he had done time, if he'd turned his life around he deserved a second chance, and I was glad that Dev was giving that to him. *If* that was his story.

I snapped back to the discussion at hand. "There should be things in the bathrooms for everybody, too. As long as they have clothes and necessities, everybody should be good. We can always order in delivery for breakfast."

"Fabulous." He grabbed my hand and started towards the stairs. "Which bedroom?" he asked. I was about to say the last on the left, and then realized that

I no longer had to stay in my room. I could stay in the master with its amazing view. Grandma Myrtle could just get over the show. I hoped she wasn't a prude.

"Let's take the master. Let everybody else fight over the others. You'll just have to protect me from the ghosts." I nudged his shoulder.

"I can do that," he said with a laugh and headed in that direction. Once safely closed inside, he turned to me as I was finishing kicking off my shoes. "You look tired," he said.

"Just what a girl wants to hear," I replied with a laugh.

He cupped my face and ran his thumb over my cheekbone. "That's not what I meant," he said and stared at me with a look that took my breath. "You are stunning. Always. I should have just come right out and said what I wanted to know."

"And what's that?" I asked.

"Are you *too* tired?"

Oh. Now I knew what he was getting at. And, hell, no, I wasn't too tired.

"For you? Never," I said, flashing him a saucy grin and a wink. And then, without another word, I turned and headed deeper into the room, removing articles of clothing as I walked and dropping them onto the floor like sensual breadcrumbs for Dev to follow.

When I made it to the bed clothed in only my red lace bra and panties and turned to face him, the look on his face made my knees weak. He hadn't moved from the entryway between the sitting room and the bedroom and stared at me with such a look of hunger on his face that I flushed from head to toe. It was a heady thing to be desired so much, and Dev's need was blatant in his expression and the tight lines of his body, not to mention the impressive erection tenting his jeans.

I gestured for him to join me, and he was in front of me in a handful of steps, somehow having discarded his T-shirt, footwear, and jeans, to appear before me in only his black boxer briefs. It was almost like magic, but I knew I had just been too mesmerized by watching the play of his muscles as he prowled to internalize what he had been doing.

"You're going to catch flies."

"Huh?" I said, meeting his gaze.

He placed a finger under my chin and applied gentle pressure, my bottom lip meeting my top. "Flies, you're going to catch flies if you keep your jaw hanging open like that." He laughed.

I shook my head with a smile. "I can't help it. You're just . . . yeah."

"You have such a way with words," he teased and winked. "But I can think of a better way for us to communicate right now."

I propped a hand on my hip and quirked a brow. "Yeah, how's that?"

"Like this." Before I knew it, I was in the air, only to come down with a bounce on the massive king-sized bed. It shocked a laugh out of me, and I looked up just in time to see Dev peeling his briefs down his muscular thighs and stepping out of them to stand between my legs. He gripped himself and stroked a few times as he stared at me, and the sight made my mouth dry. I couldn't help myself; I licked my lips and ran a hand between my breasts and down my belly, headed to where I needed to relieve some pressure, only to have him stop me.

"Uh-uh," he said, grabbing my hand gently with his. "That's my job."

He gathered both of my wrists in one of his hands and lifted my arms over my head, so my hands rested on the mattress. "Leave them there," he said and looked at me, the earnestness in his expression incredibly disarming.

And so hot.

I did as he bade me and watched as he ran a single index finger down the center of my chest to the clasp of my bra. With a quick flick of his fingers, the fastener released, and the cups fell to the sides freeing my breasts. He licked his lips. "So damn beautiful."

With gentle care, he freed me of the bra and then repositioned my hands, only the single raise of an eyebrow my command to remain where I was. I had never thought much about whether I'd like to be dominated in bed, but I found I liked it. I liked it a lot. I always felt like I had to be so strong in life. Giving myself over to someone and entrusting them with my safety and pleasure made a kaleidoscope of butterflies take flight in my belly and my breath catch.

With hands and tongue and teeth drawing a dizzying path from my neck to my toes, he freed me of the scrap of lace I wore and settled in to feast. He took me to dizzying heights I wasn't sure I'd ever come down from.

When I was nearly boneless, he reached over, protected us both, and then slid home. It wrung a gasp from me, pleasure from the depths of my soul. He moved with care, with purpose, and took me to the brink once more. Just as I was sure I couldn't take anymore, he licked up my throat and plunged deep, whispering in my ear, "Let go."

I gripped his back and screamed my release, feeling him follow me shortly after. We collapsed in a heap, panting.

"So, this is how ghosts feel," I said.

He nipped my shoulder. "What do you mean?"

"I am most definitely having an out of body experience."

He laughed and then gathered me close.

I was, without a doubt, falling in love with Deveraux Glapion.

If I hadn't already fallen.

Chapter 22

Dev

"Lark," I said into the walkie.

"Yeah, boss?" she replied, making me smile.

"Are you in the middle of something?"

"Not really. It's pretty quiet in here right now. What do you need?"

"I want to run a spirit box session if you're game."

"Always," she answered. "I'll grab the equipment and meet you in the carriage house in a few."

"Sounds great." I turned to Hanlen and explained, for both her and the audience. "A spirit box is an amazing device. It scans radio frequencies and creates white noise that the spirits can use to communicate. It's sometimes easier for them to manipulate those sounds than to build up enough energy to speak and be heard on the recorders."

"Wow, that's fascinating," she said. "I dreamed something similar earlier in the trip. How do you use it?"

"Lark and I, being the two available sensitives on the team right now since Dakota is otherwise engaged, will conduct an experiment where she wears sound-canceling headphones and a blindfold, and I ask questions through the walkie from another room. She listens to the white noise and will repeat anything she hears but she won't be able to hear us. If we're lucky, we'll get some answers to the questions we're asking."

"Oh, I can't wait to see this," Hanlen said, and I thought she was actually excited. It was always so fun to see a skeptic won over.

Lark walked through the door and shut it behind her. "Hey, guys. I brought the gear. It sucks that R2 had to leave early . . . though I hate that he's still not feeling well. He's usually such a great pack mule and saves me from lugging all the stuff." She grinned. "How do you want to do this, Dev?"

"I was thinking you should be the conduit again," I said. "Tell me anything you hear and blurt out any impressions you get."

"Sounds great. Are we trying to talk to anyone in particular?"

"Maybe," I answered. "I'm not sure I want to lead you. Are you comfortable just seeing where this goes?"

She smiled, the expression reaching her eyes. "Always."

When she was settled in a comfortable seat, and I had Hanlen move to another part of the carriage house, I settled into the corner of that room and smiled over at Hanlen. "Are you ready?" I asked her, but also Lark through the walkie.

"Putting gear on now," Lark said. We heard some shuffling over the walkie and then, "Go ahead whenever you're ready."

"Wait until you see this," I said to Hanlen.

"So ready," she answered, holding up the pen and paper she held. I had given her the task of recording what happened—my questions and any responses we got from Lark.

Into the walkie, I whispered, "Lark, can you hear me?" When I got no response, I nodded and dove in. "Who do we have with us in the carriage house?"

There still wasn't a response, so I kept going.

"Was this your house?"

"House. Died," came from the walkie. Lark's reiteration of what she heard through the headphones. "It's a male voice," she added.

"Who am I talking to?" I asked.

"Not supposed to be here," Lark said. "Who are you?"

"My name is Dev," I answered. "The woman

you're talking to is Larken. And this,"—I gestured to Hanlen—"is Hanlen Arbor. She owns this house."

"Hanlen," Lark said.

I watched as Hanlen stopped scribbling and raised her head, a look of shock on her face. I winked at her and kept going.

"Do you know Hanlen?"

"Family," Lark called. "Love."

"Holy shit," Hanlen said and kept writing.

This *was* getting good.

"You are Hanlen's family?"

"No," Lark said. The answer confused me, so I pushed a little deeper.

"No, you're not her family? Or no to something else?" Sometimes, the spirit box gave words or sentences that didn't fit with the questions asked, so you had to try and drill down a little further.

"I'm not," Lark said. "She is."

Huh . . .

"So you're not Hanlen's family but someone else here is. Okay, that's good. Who are you?"

"Soldier," Lark said through the walkie.

"You're a soldier?" I asked. "Are you who the guests refer to as The Colonel? Are you who people have seen around the property?"

"Yes," Lark said, channeling our soldier ghost. "Died here. No harm."

"You mean no harm?" I asked.

"No harm," Lark repeated.

"Good, that's good," I said. "Then why are you here? Why do you remain?" I asked.

"Like it."

"Okay, that's as good a reason as any." I laughed and looked over at Hanlen to see a smile on her face, too.

"Who is the woman with you?" I asked. "Not Larken, whoever you were talking about earlier."

"Friend," Lark said.

"Your friend?"

"Your friend," Lark said. I wasn't sure if The Colonel was echoing me or if that was an answer.

Lark came through the walkie again. "Dev, I'm seeing a beautiful woman in my head. Braids. Young. Maybe early twenties."

All right, we were getting somewhere.

"Would the woman like to come through?"

"Can't," Lark said, once again speaking for The Colonel.

"She can't?" I asked. "Why not?"

"Not able."

I wondered what could be stopping a spirit from communicating. We hadn't uncovered any malevolent entities as yet. Even the feisty one in the cold storage section was merely disruptive and a bit of a prankster. No dark energies should be keeping any others from coming through.

"Is there anything we can do to help?" I asked.

"Don't know," Lark said.

"Can we——?" Before I could even finish my sentence, I caught movement out of the corner of my eye. When I looked over, I saw a female in a leather miniskirt and a purple bustier flicker into existence, looking as solid as Hanlen and I did. Her black and purple braids hung to her waist, and even in death, she appeared more alive than a lot of people I'd seen. My breath caught, but I tried to hide my reaction.

"Okay, guys, you can tap Lark and get her out of there," I said into the walkie.

"Copy," Aaron acknowledged.

"Why'd you stop?" Hanlen asked. "That was incredible."

"We got what we needed." It was the only answer my brain would form at the moment. All I could do was stare beyond Hanlen to my cousin, watching as she gazed down at Hanlen with tears in her eyes.

I wondered if the reason she couldn't come through had to do with Hanlen. I wondered if that was why she hadn't come to talk to me. Why she'd reached out to Wren and Lark instead. I had no idea how to handle this. Hanlen had just gotten to a point where she was starting to believe—and enjoy—all of this. What would knowing that her dead best friend, the person she missed with every fiber of her being and thought of as a soul-mate sister, was standing right behind her?

I reached over and shut off my Handycam. We

could piece together footage from elsewhere later. This didn't need to be on camera.

"Hanlen, I have a serious question for you."

"Yeah?" she said, her brow wrinkling.

"If you could talk to Reagan, would you want to?"

"Yes, of course. I've always wished for that. I think it's a big reason I was so adamant that there were no such things as ghosts because I believed that she would have come to me if she still lingered."

"There are a multitude of reasons why a spirit may not be able to reach out to someone. And sometimes those reasons don't always make sense. Call it . . . universal spirit care." I laughed. "The laws require balance. And when a soul is tragically taken from this world, ripped away from those who love them, it's sometimes too hard—on both parties—for there to be contact. When that's the case, things outside of our control come into play, and no matter how strong the spirit, the person, or the medium, it just doesn't happen."

"Do you think that could be what happened with Reagan?"

I took a deep breath and let it out slowly. "I do. Hanlen, I'm going to tell you something, and I want you to try to remain calm."

"No good conversation in the history of ever started off that way."

"Fair," I answered. "But this might not be the easiest."

"I've come a long way, Dev. Is The Colonel standing behind me or something?" She turned to look behind her.

"There is a spirit behind you."

She turned back to me. "But it's not the soldier?" she asked. "Oh, God, is it a demon?"

I chuckled; I couldn't help it, especially given the look on Gunnie's face. "Not a demon." I reached over and put my hand on Hanlen's knee, brushing my thumb over her jeans. "Babe, Reagan is standing behind you."

"What?" she yelled and jumped up, only to trip on the rug and fall into my lap. I repositioned her in my arms and put my lips against her temple. "Shh, baby. It's okay."

"Okay? I'm not so sure. And . . . wait, how do you know what Reagan looks like?"

Oh, boy. This might not go over well. Then again, it wasn't like I did anything wrong. The other day just didn't seem like the right moment to explain the connection. And I needed some time to come to terms with it anyway.

"Because . . ." I swallowed hard. "Because Reagan is my cousin, Hanlen. The one I call Gunnie."

Her sharp intake of breath hit me in the solar plexus, and I struggled to breathe for a moment. Her entire body had locked, and I wasn't sure what would come next.

"Your . . . your cousin?"

"Yes. I didn't tell you the other night when you told me her name because I needed a beat to wrap my head around it. She's another special thing that you and I share. Yet another reason that I think we were meant to be in each other's lives."

"But . . . I don't understand," she said.

"I know. But she's here. And she's here for a reason. The Colonel said that she couldn't communicate for some reason but that she was here because of her family. Someone she loves. That's both of us."

Hanlen sat up straighter on my lap and pulled her hair back, tugging at the strands. I could almost see her trying to make sense of what she'd just heard. When she looked to where Reagan stood, my heart skipped a beat.

"Goddamn you, Ray," she said, taking both me and Gunnie by surprise, if the look on my cousin's face was anything to go by. "How could you leave me like that? I know you didn't have a choice, but if you can be here now, you could have been there for me then. Could have been there all these years." Tears ran freely down her face, and I felt the sobs in her body. "I know it's not your fault but I . . . I can't do this right now. This will have to wait. I need a goddamn drink." She flew off my lap, her sobs echoing in the room in her wake, and was gone before I could even think of a word to say to keep her there. When I heard the door slam, I looked back at my cousin.

"What is going on, Gunnie?"

She shrugged, pointed to her lips, shook her head, and then pointed to her ears before shrugging again. Something was keeping her from being heard. At least, by me. I was probably lucky to be seeing her right now.

"Have you tried reaching out and talking to me?"

She nodded.

"When did this all start?"

She pointed in the direction Hanlen had gone.

"When Hanlen arrived?"

She nodded again.

Interesting . . . I thought about the necklace Hanlen wore.

"Does it have anything to do with her veve?"

She cocked her head and seemed to think for a minute then held her thumb and forefinger about an inch apart before shrugging again.

Maybe a little.

"Have you learned anything about your murder?"

She shook her head and then stared off to where Hanlen had gone again, a look of wistfulness in her expression.

"I felt soul magick in that pendant. Was that you? Did you do it recently? After death? It felt like departed power."

She nodded again.

Well, that explained the strength and unusual feeling of the protection ward. My cousin had been a very strong practitioner back in the day, despite her age, and even though she'd had to keep it under wraps given the stigma of such things even as recently as ten years ago—even from those closest to her. Even in death, she would be able to work powerful magic. Which made her not being able to communicate properly extra infuriating.

"I'll get to the bottom of this, sweets," I said, and watched as she nodded once more, tears glistening in her ethereal eyes again. "Will you be back?"

She moved her head in agreement and then gestured to herself, crossing her arms over her chest before pointing at me and then outside. She would be back because she loved us.

"Love you, too, Gun. So much. I've missed you."

She pointed to herself, held up two fingers—she missed me, too—then blew me a kiss and disappeared.

I had a show to finish, but I also had to find Hanlen and make sure she was okay. The rest of the team could take care of things for a little bit.

Chapter 23

"To feel another's life force as powerfully as your own, that is love."
~Marty Rubin

She walked out the door, and he stood, transfixed. She was the most beautiful thing he had ever seen. From the time he'd first seen her dancing in the club all those years ago, he'd known he wanted to engage in a communion of blood and soul. He wanted her in him. Needed to possess her—make her his.

And when she rolled back into town, and he saw her again, everything came crashing back. His darkness roiled, seeking and searching sustenance of the one being he felt would be his salvation, the one with the light his darkness was drawn to. He took it as a sign that this was his moment. This was the sacrifice and offering he had been looking for to make his other half happy.

The one that got away.

He took in her body language from across the way. She seemed upset. While he knew now that fear was like sweet ambrosia, and defeated acquiescence was tart like lemonade, he imagined anger would be like the best gumbo, spicy and kicking, warming him from the inside.

He could so easily sneak up on her right now and snatch her, take her back to his lair and give her the eternal kiss, set her free, make her his in both body and, eventually, soul. Break her mind and take possession of that, as well. But it didn't feel right. He wanted it to be perfect.

Somehow, he knew that the moment would present itself tonight. Maybe not now, but later, for sure, she *would* be his. He would finally be able to look her in the eyes. He would *finally* be seen. Because he knew she would see him. And while he knew the cops believed that giving him an identity would remove his power, to him, it would only make him a god.

Chapter 24

Hanlen

I didn't know what to do with myself. Pacing the carriage house's balcony and tugging at my hair, taking long drags from the flask, I tried to get myself under control. This was pain. It wasn't truly anger, even though it presented itself that way. I didn't understand any of this stuff. Maybe Ray had a good reason for not being able to let me know that she was fine. And Dev hadn't kept the information from me about him being related to her on purpose, he simply didn't think it was the right time to spill those particular beans. And I got that. I really did. Still, my heart and my head hurt, and I didn't know what to do about any of it.

I heard the French doors behind me open and felt a presence at my back. I knew who it was.

"Are you okay?" Dev asked, his voice like melted chocolate.

"I don't know," I answered, being truthful. "This is a lot, Dev. When I came back to town, I didn't believe in any of this. And while I can't discount anything I've seen and experienced, having it shoved in my face like this in such a personal way is a lot to take in."

"I know," he said. "That's why I didn't say anything the other night when you told me Reagan's full name. It just felt too . . . overwhelming. Even for me. I knew I'd get a chance to talk to you about it all later. But I didn't expect Gunnie to be here."

I rubbed my hands up and down opposite arms. "Yeah, I know. I do. Doesn't mean my emotions aren't all over the place."

"I get that, too. I want to know what happened to her as much as you do. And it sucks that we can't just get those answers. I want that almost as much as I want to find out who murdered my sister and stop this sicko from picking off people I care about. That *you* care about."

"Fucking asshole." It was the only thing I could think to say, and it felt right in the moment. Good. I turned to Dev, and the look in his eyes disarmed me.

"I'm sorry," he said. And I knew he meant it.

"You really don't have anything to apologize for.

I'm sorry I stormed out of there. It was just a bit much. Did I ruin the shoot?"

"Not at all," he assured me and moved closer, pulling me against his chest. I sighed and wrapped my arms around him, soaking in his strength. "Everybody else is still working, and the final product is the result of a bunch of careful editing to piece all the bits together into a narrative. We'll get more footage later, too. It'll all be good." He kissed my head. "Promise."

I pulled back a bit to look up at him. "Are you sure?"

He tucked my hair behind my ear as he so often did, and goosebumps erupted on my skin. "Absolutely. I should probably get back in there, though. We still have some things I need to finish up tonight in the main house. Are you all right?"

I rubbed my hands over my head, smoothing my hair back, and turned to look out at the yard and the manor. "I'm fine. You should get back to it. I just need a few minutes to compose myself if that's all right. Did Ray leave?"

"She did. Something's going on with her. She can't communicate with me right now, and that's never happened before. I'll have to get to the bottom of it later. Actually . . ." He seemed nervous all of a sudden.

"What?" I asked.

"Would you mind if I borrowed your necklace for a bit? I'd like to see if me using it as a trigger object will help Larken and me tap into Gunnie's energy better and speak with her. If it works, I promise we'll come and get you immediately."

I shrugged. "Sure. Of course. Just don't lose it." I pulled it over my head and puddled it in his outstretched palm.

"Thanks. It's safe with me," he said and tipped up my chin. With a lingering look, his ocean-water pools took me in, and I felt my muscles loosen. He leaned in to kiss me, and I knew in that moment that he was mine. And I was his . . . if he'd have me.

"I'd better get," he said. "Are you going to be okay? Be able to make it back to the main house all right yourself once you're ready?"

"Yeah, I'm good. Get. I'll see you in a few." I rose on tiptoe and kissed him again, the words I wanted to say on the tip of my tongue. But it didn't feel like the right time. I could tell him later when we were alone. When we could talk about it, and I could better gauge his mood and response. We had a lot of things to talk about if he was receptive to us being together, but that all could wait.

For now.

He ran his hand from my shoulder to my palm and let my fingers slip through his as he walked away, severing our connection at the very last moment. I hugged myself again and watched him go and then turned back to the woods, looking at the trees and the moon high in the sky.

This trip had been one of many discoveries. Not the least of which was the core of who I was. I'd started this journey as a single-minded, jaded skeptic with no desire to be anything more and no care for what people thought of me, to someone who was now coming to believe in things beyond explanation and searched out human connection.

I waited another few minutes with some deep breathing and a few more sips of whiskey for courage, then headed downstairs and out the back door of the carriage house.

Just as I was rounding the corner, I felt a sharp pain in the back of my head, and my legs slipped out from under me. I saw the grass rushing up with dizzying speed as the flask fell from my fingers to clatter on the pavers.

I was out before my head hit the ground.

―――

I WOKE to the smell of rot and mildew, mold and decay, and the feel of cold, rough stone under my body. Before I even opened my eyes, I knew where I was—the Arbor family cemetery, which rested just behind Bea and August's cottage.

When I finally cracked my lids, searing pain ricocheted through my skull, bringing a surge of bile and Evan Williams apple to my throat. I went to reach for my mouth and realized that I was restrained. I tried to calm my heart rate, steady my breathing, but panic was steadily creeping in, becoming its own monster ready to overtake me.

When I steadied enough that I knew I wouldn't throw up all over myself and possibly die from drowning in my own vomit, I slowly turned my head to see someone standing in front of a raised platform, their back to me. I couldn't make out features or details in the dim light and through my blurry vision, but I got the sense that it was someone large—at least much larger than me.

"What do you want from me?" I asked, with more confidence than I felt.

"Ah, you're awake. Wonderful," they said. It was a *he*. Or at least it sounded like a male. I probably shouldn't make assumptions. I mean, it was the least of my concerns. But they still didn't turn around to face me, just kept doing whatever it was they were doing.

I felt a shiver rush down my body and a feeling of dread took up root in my belly. This wasn't good. And I wasn't even sure if anybody had examined the crypts yet. Would they even think to look for me here whenever they realized I was missing?

"I'm sorry I had to hit you so hard, but we were running out of time for me to get you out of there safely."

"Sure, yeah, you're forgiven. Now, just let me go. We can forget it ever happened."

"But that's not how this works, *cher*. You've been destined for me, for *us*, for a very long time. I was sure of that the first time I saw you. Call it . . . intuition. Honestly, it's past time we established that."

What the fuck is this person talking about?

"Uh, do I know you?"

"Mmm, kinda."

That voice. I knew that voice. Why did I know that voice? From where? I tried to shuffle through my memories but all it did was cause my head to hurt worse and nausea to roll through me.

"You know," he said conversationally, as if we were sitting down for coffee, "that night all those years ago has never left my thoughts. You in that sexy black-and-red number, your crimson-streaked hair shining in the strobes, your body moving to the music."

My blood turned to ice. I remembered that outfit. The way my hair had been back then. A decade ago. The night Reagan had been killed.

Oh. My. God.

"I knew I wanted you even back then, *cher*. We wanted to assimilate. Show you the way. But then you took off, and I was left with your friend. Now, don't get me wrong, she was sweet. Her blood like sour candy on the tongue, but she wasn't who I wanted. Not really. However, she was my first, so she will always be special. I didn't actually mean to take her life. I only wanted to share in it with her. But things went too far. I feel guilt that I didn't have a coin to give her like I do my sacrifices now. Especially since she basically started this little adventure for me. She deserved better." He continued messing with something on the raised platform. I saw what looked like tubes and a flash of metal.

Holy motherfucking shit. This was the serial killer. This was RƎDRΩM. And he was the asshole who had taken Ray from me, who had stolen August from Bea, who had killed my mark. This was the depraved son of a bitch who'd cut Dev's twin's life short, thus stealing Findley's, as well. This was the psychopath who'd viciously murdered Burke and who knew how many others.

I wanted to kill *him* with my bare hands.

"What the hell is wrong with you?" I asked, my entire body shaking. "How can you be so . . . evil?"

"Oh, come now, *cher*. All those my shadow-self becomes obsessed with play an important role in the circle of life. They are all important—in this life and the next. But I know now that all of them were to lead me to you. It's divine guidance. And the fact that everything ties back to you in some way is very telling, don't you think? I didn't realize it until recently. But when I had the epiphany, I knew. I just *knew*. This was all meant to be."

He turned to me then, and the light of the lantern on the corner of the slab hit his face. The electricity and ice-water rush of adrenaline flashed through my veins so fast it locked my breath in my lungs.

Holy hell.

It was . . .

He sketched a bow.

Fucking Remy Dee Reaume.

The RƎDRΩM made so much more sense now.

Heeeere's Remy.

Son of a bitch.

Chapter 25

Dev

"That's a wrap, guys," I said into the walkie. Everybody chimed in that they understood and went about their tasks for the end of the night, making sure that everything was ready for tomorrow. We'd had a great investigation. Lark, Hanlen, and I had contacted The Colonel, Dakota had gotten indisputable evidence that our lady in the broomstick skirt and the head scarves was indeed Chloe Aillet, and without much trying, Padre and Sky had recorded additional EVP evidence of our woman in white, Myrtle Arbor. We'd had no interaction with the child ghost—I didn't think there was actually one here, honestly.

We had some additional research to do and a ton

of video evidence to review—things we'd caught on the SLS camera when it picked up and mapped anomalies, making anything that we couldn't see with the naked eye appear as a stick figure on the recording, and some variances in the thermal camera footage, not to mention our static night-vision cameras—but all in all, it had been a great night.

I saw Lark walk into the room, wrapping a cable around her hand and elbow to loop it. "Good one tonight, huh?" she asked.

"It absolutely was. So, I have a question."

"Shoot," she said and set her equipment in the box before turning to me.

"You've spoken with Gunnie before and know who she is, but do you know what she looks like?"

"Mmm, you know what? I don't think I do. I'm not sure I've ever gotten a psychic picture of her when she's reached out."

"The woman you saw earlier during our spirit box session? That was my cousin."

"The hottie with the purple braids?"

I smiled. "That would be her."

"Wow. So why was the soldier talking about her? Or wasn't he? You pulled me out and were deep in conversation with Hanlen before I could ask how the whole spirit box session went and see whether anything made sense with the communication."

"As you're aware, she's been having some trouble reaching out. We're not sure why. You couldn't hear her as clearly as you had before—or as you do with others—and she hasn't come to me at all lately. And while I saw her tonight, she couldn't talk to me. She indicated that it all started when Hanlen came to town."

"Hanlen?" Lark asked. "Why would that be?"

I sighed and cracked my neck. "I wish I knew. But do you remember the other night at Lafitte's when Hanlen briefly mentioned the best friend she'd lost and said that's why she left the city a decade ago?"

"Now that you mention it, actually, yeah, I do. Her sorrow was palpable."

"Well, that best friend . . . it was my cousin. Gunnie to me, Reagan—or rather, Ray—to Hanlen. Seems we have yet another connection."

"Wow, that's wild," Lark said and took a seat on the nearest chair. "Did you tell Hanlen that she was here tonight?"

"Yeah, I did." I took a seat on the couch opposite her. "She was upset, as expected. It's like ripping open an old wound without anesthetic. But she said she would be okay. And it sort of forced her to believe, you know? So maybe that's a good thing. I dunno. I'm hopeful that maybe she'll let me do the spell that will allow her to see and talk to Gunnie temporarily. But . . ." I said and trailed off.

"But what?" Lark asked.

"I think we need to try and speak to her first. Gunnie, I mean. Hanlen gave me her necklace to use as a trigger object. I figured she'd be fine with the protections you and I put on the place. The veve used to be my cousin's, and it's full of magic—both residual and departed soul magick. I was wondering if you'd be willing to add your power to mine to see if we can break through whatever is going on. I have a feeling it might be backfired intention. That the protective magic on the necklace is protecting Hanlen—and in a way, me—from something it perceives as danger."

Lark reached out and put her hand over mine where it rested on my knee. "Of course, Dev. Absolutely. Let's do it."

We set our intentions and settled in, facing each other over a lit candle. I held the veve, while Lark grasped the chain, and we called upon my cousin.

She flickered into existence in the corner. I looked up at her and smiled, and she returned the expression.

"Hey, Gun," I said. "Think you can try talking to us again with Lark here?" Her lips moved but I still didn't hear anything. When I looked at Lark, I saw her concentrating, her eyes closed.

"She . . ." Lark started. "She's here."

"Yeah, she is. She's standing right over your shoulder, but I still can't hear her."

"I can," Lark said, "but it's still kind of muffled. A little better, but definitely not super clear. Um . . . she said . . . she said she thinks we need to do an illumination spell. Something about the protection ward on the veve having backfired a bit, just like you said."

I nodded. It really did make a weird kind of sense. If the magic was meant to protect, and it saw something as a potential threat, it would repel it. And Hanlen being faced with her dead best friend after so many years of anguish would definitely cause harm. Or, at the very least, plenty of hurt. Enough to warrant activation of the protective magics. And given my connection to Hanlen, it also made a strange sort of sense why I had been included in that.

"Okay. That's easy enough. Wrap your hand around mine." Lark did as instructed. "Now, just concentrate on my words and add your intention."

She took a deep breath and let it out slowly as if centering herself, and I did the same. I said the words for the spell and was just about to tell Gunnie to try to communicate again, when Wren and Findley popped into the room, looking frantic and terrified.

"Dev, get to the cemetery."

"The cemetery? What do you mean?"

"No questions. Now, get there now, brother."

"Noooooo." I heard that. Gunnie's wail. And just as quickly as the sound registered, she disappeared.

"What the fuck?" Lark said.

I couldn't agree more.

"Dev, man. We gotta move," Findley urged. "Cemetery."

"We haven't even been out there yet. Why would I need to go out there?"

"Less talk, more action," Wren said, flapping her hands. "We'll meet you there."

And then the couple disappeared. I took the chain from Lark and stuffed both it and the pendant into my pocket.

"What the hell's going on, Dev? Was that your cousin? That shriek?"

"Yeah, it was. I even heard it. Seems our spell worked. My sister was here with Findley, too. They said I have to get to the cemetery immediately."

"I didn't hear them," Lark said.

"I don't know what's going on. Can you gather up the troops and let them know what happened? I gotta get over there and see what's up."

"Yeah, yeah. Of course," Lark said. "We'll meet you there. Go."

I exited the house as fast as I could and tore across the property, headed for the cemetery I'd seen the first day when Hanlen had given me a tour. It was so old that I knew there were spirits there, and we'd decided not to investigate it unless it tied to something we uncovered at the house or the carriage house. We hadn't even included it in the circle when we set up, especially after everything that happened with August and the fact that it was butted up against that crime scene. Why in the world would I need to go out there? And why were Wren and Findley so upset? Not to mention, why had Gunnie sounded so anguished?

When I rounded the bend, I saw Wren, Findley,

Desmond, and Gunnie standing around the cemetery's biggest mausoleum, thought to hold the remains of the family's matriarch and patriarch, the first of the line who started Arborwood. They were a bit away from the structure, their hands raised, and I wondered why.

The frantic look on my sister's face when she turned to me was enough to make my stomach drop, and I still had no idea what exactly was going on.

I approached cautiously. "What's this all about, guys?" The rest of them turned to me, as well. When I saw the spectral tears coursing down Gunnie's face, I knew something bad was going on and was afraid to find out what. My instincts were screaming but I couldn't get a lock on the feelings or impressions.

"It's Hanlen, Dev. He's got Hanlen," Findley said, seeming to be the only one who could get a handle on themselves enough to reply.

My stomach bottomed out, and I felt a rush of fear swamp me, stealing my breath and making the ground under me sway for a moment. "What are you talking about?"

Desmond pointed at the structure. "She's in there. He has her tied to a vault. And we can't get in. Can't even get close. None of us can. Something is stopping us from entering. We tried. I'm not sure what we could have done, but . . ."

"You need to help her, Dev. Please," Gunnie pleaded, and I started at the sound of her voice. When I looked at her, the look on her face about sent me to my knees again. I had no idea who this *he* was that they were talking about, but it didn't matter. If Hanlen was in trouble, I would move Heaven and Earth to get her to safety.

I surged forward and to the side of the structure, hurrying to the little window. Whatever was keeping the ghosts from getting close didn't seem to affect me, at least not entirely. Though I *did* feel something. I needed to get a better picture of what was going on before I barged in, metaphorical guns-blazing, so I peeked inside but couldn't see much around the angel statue situated right in front of the opening. I did see candlelight, long shadows dancing across the stone, stretching like skeletal fingers. I stopped to listen for a minute but heard only scuffling coming from inside. I wished that one of them would talk so I would know that Hanlen was still okay and could maybe get a better feel for who was in there with her and what I needed to do next. I pounded on the invisible barrier, my stomach in knots, and then yelled to the others.

"Who has her? What the hell is going on? I can't see anything."

Wren burst into tears. "It's RƎDRΩM. Oh, sweet lwas. We heard him talking earlier. It's the asshole who killed me and August. Burke. The others. He also admitted to killing Reagan." She stopped for a minute, sobs wracking her body as she looked over at our cousin. "Said she was his first but that he really wanted Hanlen. Saints, Dev. We . . ." She hiccuped. "We can't let him take Hanlen, too."

Holy fuck.

I threw my shoulder into the invisible barrier, again and again, trying to get inside yet attempting to think of the best way to handle this. I didn't know if he was armed. I assumed he would be, but with what? And how efficient would he be with it? Was he only good when his prey was unaware and helpless? Or did he know how to fight? How big was he? How old? There were so many unanswered questions, and I didn't want to put Hanlen in more danger than she already was. The ghosts couldn't scout for me to get the lay of the land before I rushed in, and I couldn't get a good enough visual inside to see what was going on. Not to mention, I didn't know what else might be set up to keep me out. There was *something* but I couldn't pin it down.

Just as I was considering trying the other side of the structure in hopes there might be another window slit, a scream rent the air, sending every hair on my body to attention, and filling my veins with fizz. I rushed towards the front and forward, ready to barge in somehow, personal safety be damned, only to hit a stronger invisible wall and be thrown back several feet, coming to land on my back, the ground knocking the wind from my lungs.

"*Ooomph.*" I lay there for a moment, trying to

catch my breath and regain my senses, my instincts screaming at me.

Most definitely something else in place here.

What the fucking hell just happened? *How?*

I looked up to see a huddle of people surrounding me, all with concerned and terrified looks on their faces, though none of them able to assist. They couldn't touch me. They couldn't help.

I sat up and blew out a breath, shaking my head slightly and taking stock of my body. Nothing broken. But I didn't feel all that great, and it had really slowed me down. Whatever that shield was packed a wallop. The strangest thing? It felt almost familiar. Like my magic, yet . . . not. Bastardized somehow. How was that even possible?

I finally jumped to my feet and looked at those surrounding me. "Do you guys feel that?" I asked.

"Yeah," Wren said. "When we first got here and weren't able to even get close, it was really confusing because it kind of reminded me of you. At first, I thought I maybe misunderstood my calling to come here, and that you were with Hanlen in there. But when Gunnie popped up, screaming, I knew that wasn't the case. And then we heard him."

"He went on and on about how she was supposed to be his. How she would belong to him," Findley added.

"I have to get in there," I said to no one in partic-ular, tugging at my hair. Lark was supposed to be bringing some help. But I wasn't sure I could wait. Another scream ripped through the still night air and tore a hole in my heart. Fucking hell.

I ran closer again, throwing magic at whatever was keeping me from Hanlen, urgency yet caution riding me and making me a bit woozy. Then I stopped, standing with arms outstretched to search for the source of the magic. There had to be some sort of . . . something to power it. Even I couldn't work a spell like this without a charm or some kind of correspondence. I frantically looked and felt every-where—on the ground, on the façade, in the trees. I didn't see anything, but that didn't mean much. It was dark as shit out here and all I had was my mini flashlight.

Just as I was about to risk a run at the door again, I heard pounding footfalls against the grass and looked up in time to see Lark, James, Padre, Sky, and Dakota rounding the bend. Hope surged for a moment, making me lightheaded for a second. I ran over.

"What's going on?" Lark asked. "My psychic warnings are out of control right now. I couldn't find Aaron or Jeremy."

"A fucking psychopathic serial killer has Hanlen," I answered, needing them to know what was going on but worried we'd waste too much time if they asked questions. "But there's some sort of magic shield around the place. Something none of us can break through. It literally threw me back several feet when I tried to storm through the door."

"Oh, sweet goddess," Lark breathed. "What do you need? What can we do?"

"Dev?" Wren called, and I looked over. I jogged to her and looked where she was pointing. There, on the ground, right where they were all stuck, was a line of dirt and . . . oh, shit. Black salt. The most powerful banishing correspondence out there, especially if the right sea salt was used. Combine that with graveyard dirt and the right intention, and it was no wonder we were having so much trouble.

Fuck.

"Lark!" I yelled. She came running over and looked down where I pointed, to where my flashlight shone. "Oh, damn. That's not good." She looked up, shaking her head at me. "No wonder it kicked your ass. Who do we know that can do magic like this? It feels almost . . . I don't know. Familiar somehow."

"Yeah, it does. Because it's my fucking magic. Sort of. It's twisted, not quite right, but it's mine. I just have no idea how." I looked around the area, not sure why but hoping that I'd get some flash of inspiration. I needed to get in there. I had to save Hanlen. Just as I had that thought, another scream split the night, shattering my heart right along with it.

"God Almighty," Padre said, crossing himself and whispering prayers as everybody else went on alert, the urgency ramping up another notch.

"Lark, Dakota," I said, calling the women over. "Wren, Reagan, Findley," I gestured for the ghosts. "We need to do this together. I need you all to use your combined power, magic, and intention to break through this barrier. I need to get in there to Hanlen. Now."

"Use your love, Dev," Wren said and reached out to me. I wished she could touch me. I would have loved a hug and some strength right about now. But she was right. I loved Hanlen, and love was the most powerful magic of all.

"Lord and Lady, spirits, ancestors, guides and friends, assist us this night to bring evil an end. Lend us your strength of three times three, this is my will, so mote it be," Lark chanted.

Surprisingly, I heard Sky whisper-echo Lark's last words and felt a flare of power in my chest. Interesting, but not something I could dwell on right now. She joined Padre, slipping her hand into his as he said the Lord's Prayer. She wasn't actually praying but lending him her strength, her stalwart belief in science and energy that was magic in itself. I then focused on the others.

I heard Gunnie and Wren chanting from their corner of the mausoleum, hands clasped. Findley walked around the building's side to join in with Lark, their histories and beliefs more aligned, as Findley had been part of a local coven before his death. I heard Lark gasp, likely hearing and feeling Fin lend her his magic. We stood in a triskele formation around the structure, and I hoped the sacred geometry would work in our favor, as well.

"Keep it up. I'm going to get close. I'll bet there's another layer of protection at the door. If you guys can weaken the outer layer and then move forward, I think I can break the physical line and then muscle my way in. Especially since this is, in essence, *my* magic."

I both felt and heard the work ramping up behind me, and it gave me some confidence. I only hoped that the silence that reigned once again from inside was a good sign, an indication that he wasn't currently hurting Hanlen. And not a bad one, meaning she could no longer make sounds.

When I reached the door, I heard Lark call over the din of voices. "Now, Dev. Do it now! We still can't get through, but you should be able to. Go."

I scraped my boot through the line of dirt and salt that was at the entrance to the mausoleum and felt the magic snap, like a rubber band stretched too far. I felt much the same.

When the vacuum of power hit me, I barreled through the door until the magic stopped me in my tracks for a minute again. Fuming and frantic, I took in the sight before me in a blink. Hanlen was tied to the tomb, her arms secured at her sides and her feet tied to the bottom. She looked conscious, but barely. I saw blood trickling from wounds at her neck and on her arms, some sort of contraption positioned to capture the blood as it ran free. When I glanced up, I saw someone in the shadows over by another tomb, turning toward me. I caught the glint of metal in lantern and candlelight and allowed my gaze to travel from the hand up the arm to the shoulder, neck, and finally the face.

The look was pure evil. No feeling. No empathy. Just blank entitlement. But outside of that, despite the fact that the look alone gave me shivers, I felt my body lock when my brain finally caught up to what was going on and I was able to process what I was seeing.

Because I knew that face. I didn't recognize the look on it, but I knew those eyes, that mouth, those cheekbones.

I had seen them nearly every day for the last five years.

"Hello, Dev," he sneered, before taking a sip from a goblet and looking up at me. He wiped a macabre Kool-Aid stain from his mouth with a finger before sucking the digit and letting it go with a pop, a chilling smile on his face.

I shuddered.

"Remy, what the hell?"

Chapter 26

Hanlen

My head felt as if it were stuffed with cotton, and the taste of metal coated my tongue. I felt every injury like a second painful pulse, both in time with my heartbeat and seemingly separate from it. Remy had manhandled me a bit and then made incisions at my neck and wrists, attaching some sort of device and tubes to drain me, babbling all along about how it was an honor; how he would never choose anybody else for something so special.

Fucking psychopath.

I felt my strength waning with each breath, and figured I must be hallucinating when I swore I saw Dev enter the crypt. I was having trouble keeping my eyes open, but I took some deep breaths to try and center myself and bring me back to reality. I was just about to admit to myself that maybe I wasn't as okay as I wanted to believe when I still saw Dev. Until Remy spoke up.

"Hello, Dev."

Oh my God, he was actually here. When I took another deep breath and concentrated, I thought I heard voices from outside, too. Dev hadn't come alone. Maybe we could make it through this. Remy had seriously cracked. Or maybe he'd always been this way and was just really good at pretending to be so-called normal. When I took a moment to think about that harder, I realized that he was likely never quote-unquote normal. If he'd killed Reagan, that was ten years ago. Remy had to be years younger than me. Which would mean that he had only been a teenager back then. I thought back to the club we'd been to that night and realized that it had been an eighteen-and-over venue—the kind that gave wristbands at the door for anyone twenty-one and older. He very well could have been there and still been in high school. All of this was bad enough, but to know that he'd been like this and had made his first kill at that young of an age . . . it was almost more disturbing.

The private investigator in me was fascinated by the psychology of it all. What made a person that way? What had broken in Remy at such a young age that it had warped his mind and turned him into a person who could so callously take another human's life? And then to take that a step further and feel— legitimately *believe*—that he was doing it for a good reason. For something that was beneficial to all. Because he really did believe that. I read people for a living, and I could tell that he truly believed what he had been saying when he was spewing his nonsense about honor and privilege and gifts. How did that even happen?

I tried to bring myself back to the present.

"Remy, what the hell?" Dev said, his words and tone full of vitriol.

"I'm sorry you had to see this, Dev. I know that you developed an attachment to Hanlen, but she was never yours. She's always been mine. Since that night so long ago when I saw her dancing and knew she was my salvation."

"Listen, man," Dev said, regulating his tone and assuming a non-threatening posture. "We can get you some help. We can figure this out. Just let her go. Let me go. Let me help her."

Remy cocked his head and stared at Dev, his expression containing a look I couldn't decipher. "Let her go?" he asked. "Why would I want to do that? She's mine. As I said, she's always been mine. Her life force will revitalize me and let me be reborn. Will soothe the darkness inside me. I will no longer have to walk in the shadows, a slave to my darker side. I will once again be part of the light like I was as a child. Before it took control, whispering in my ear."

What the ever-loving-hell?

"And she will be free. Free of the hurt and pain and heartache of life. I will send her on her way to Paradise, a coin in hand for the ferryman. She can finally reunite with Reagan. When she told us the story of her loss the night of the cast party, I knew that I needed to help her. I could feel her pain and knew exactly how I could fix things. I could let her see her friend again, and she could help me *become*. I never thought I'd get the chance, despite all my efforts to make it happen, but fate brought her back to me. The minute I saw her, I knew that this was meant to be. Everything fell into place too perfectly for me to have any doubts. She's the light I've searched for."

"Fucking hell, Remy," Dev said and scrubbed his hands over his head and face. "What the actual fuck?"

"You just don't understand. And I don't expect you to." He moved forward to lean over me as he talked to Dev.

"The magic. How did you do it?" Dev asked as he waved his hands in complicated patterns. I assumed he was trying to free himself from whatever Remy had done to keep him away.

"Oh, that?" Remy said and laughed. "Well, that's all thanks to you. I watch you, you know. I learn. And that time we had that cast party at the Vodou temple, and you taught us all a little simple magic to get a rise out of the super twins, Harper, and Sky? I knew I could do it. I just knew that with enough work and practice and some supplies carefully obtained from you and Birdie, I could do whatever I wanted. Especially after I'd fed. It's such a rush, Dev. Like pure, unfiltered life flowing through your veins. Add in the magic, and I've never felt so powerful. I'm becoming a god."

Jesus, this guy was a mess. I wasn't sure there was hope for him. Even with professional help.

"Just let her go, man. Let Hanlen go, and we'll get you the help you need."

"I don't *need* help!" Remy yelled. "I am exactly where I'm supposed to be, doing exactly what I was meant to do. I think it's you who doesn't belong." He pointed the knife at Dev, and my heart rate picked up, making every wound on my body throb even more. Despite the lethargy overtaking me, I fought to stay awake. To stay alert and figure out a way out of this. What in the hell was everybody outside waiting for? Why weren't they rushing in to save the day?

I saw Dev raise his hands and fling them out, then walk closer to Remy's side of the crypt I lay on. He must have been able to get through whatever Remy had done. I wanted to tell him not to go. Wished he'd just save himself. I imagined the worst-case scenarios that may unfold if Dev took Remy on, one-on-one. Remy was much larger than Dev, and while Dev wasn't old by any stretch of the imagination, he *was* older than Remy. And Remy had adrenaline and a god-complex on his side besides. Not to mention, he an utterly psycopath.

Just as I was about to force myself to tell Dev to stop, he sprang, knocking into Remy and pile-driving him back against the tomb behind them. Remy grunted and brought an elbow down on Dev's back, causing the air to rush out of Dev's lungs in a whoosh. Dev recovered and tried to take Remy to the ground, only to be shoved off and punched in the face. Dev's head snapped to the side, but he somehow remained standing and kicked at Remy, catching the other man in the midsection and sending him back once again.

Remy slashed out with the dagger, the blade glinting in the low light. As if in slow motion, I heard the swish of steel against fabric, undercut by a squelching sound of severed flesh that turned my stomach. When Dev drew in a sharp inhale, I knew he'd been cut, but I wasn't sure where. They were too far away from me now. And being restrained and weak, I couldn't lift my head enough to catch more than vague impressions of what was going on.

I felt so helpless. The man I loved was battling for his life. Fighting for *mine*. And I couldn't do anything to help. I tried to pull against my bonds, but I was too weak, couldn't even free myself an inch. Grunts and dull thuds continued as the two fought, and I worried that Remy would hit something vital in Dev with that knife. But would I even be alive to find out? I felt my body giving in to defeat. Saw the shadows creeping in at the edges of my vision. Just as I was about to say something, at least tell Dev how I felt before I died, I caught movement out of the corner of my eye and saw a commotion at the door.

I turned my head to see Larken, James, Paxton, Dakota, and Schuyler rush through the door, the latter holding a gun.

Was I imagining things?

"Freeze, motherfucker," she called and pointed the handgun at the grappling pair, her stance steady and aim true. The guys stopped fighting long enough to look up, and I finally heard the blade hit the stone and skitter across the surface. Dev must have disarmed Remy in his surprise.

Just as I was about to relax, I saw more movement near the door and looked over, only to have my stomach drop and my breath freeze in my lungs. Four people entered, but it was the one in the front that metaphorically stopped me in my tracks. Black and purple braids that hung to her waist. A leather miniskirt and a bustier. Glowing umber skin.

Reagan.

It was Ray.

And I could *see* her.

Until everything went black.

Chapter 27

Dev

It took maybe five minutes from the time the gang finally entered the mausoleum before Remy was face-down on the stone floor, his hands and feet secured with zip ties that James had in his pocket from wrapping up and securing the equipment.

After checking on Hanlen and making sure Lark had her, I turned to the petite, raven-haired woman standing next to me, her aim still true on Remy as he lay on the ground, her stance easy and loose. I gently reached over and placed my hand on hers, exerting just a bit of pressure to let her know it was okay to lower the gun. "Sky, you can relax."

It was like someone had flipped a switch. Her

posture changed and she rubbed the heel of her hand still holding the gun against her forehead and hair. "What the fuck? What the actual ever-loving fuck?" She flipped a switch on the side of the gun and lowered it to her side, still full of frenetic energy—I could see it sparking through her aura. She paced, wiping the palm of her free hand on her jeans as she did.

I looked up at the rest of the crew. Everybody had had some pretty creative things to say when they saw who held Hanlen, and I was afraid I'd have to hold a few of them back from actually trying to kill him. As it was, James still knelt with his knee in Remy's back—probably none too gently—the bigger man struggling but not able to do much given the way he was restrained. We couldn't hear the bullshit he spewed either, since Lark had ripped off the silk scarf she wore almost immediately and threw it to James to tie it around his head as a gag and then went straight to Hanlen to do a quick healing spell. It wouldn't be enough to heal her completely, but it *would* give her some relief and stabilize her until we could get her some medical attention.

I caught Padre crossing himself again and figured it was his way of dealing with the evil we had been confronted with. One of our own—someone we had worked with for five seasons of our show, cared about, treated as family—was a deranged serial killer. He'd murdered two of my family members and one of my friends. Had stolen a sick and elderly man from his wife and Hanlen. He'd drained Dustin Reynolds and who knew how many others and left them to rot in the city. And all for what? To . . . *become*? Whatever the hell that meant.

I looked at Wren and Findley wrapped in each other's embrace and wondered what this meant for them. For us. Would they remain on this side of the veil, or would they finally cross over? The evil had a name now. A face. His power was gone. He would be spending the rest of his life behind bars—if a jury of his peers didn't give him the death penalty. I could see a good defense lawyer trying to use an insanity plea to get him off, but he was lucid and totally in control, and that was scarier than anything.

I couldn't think about that right now. Snapping out of my shock and seeing that Remy was contained, I finally rushed to Hanlen. Lark had untied her and removed the blood-draining device, but she still hadn't regained consciousness.

"We called the police and an ambulance," Dakota said as she came up next to Lark. "They should be here soon."

"Good, that's good," I said, not sure what else to say. I brushed Hanlen's hair away from her face and took in her pale complexion and the cuts and bruises Remy had left on her body—one of which was deep enough that Lark had said she was afraid to stop putting pressure on it. I wanted to murder him. I wanted to beat him to a bloody pulp for even daring to touch her. To harm her. She was *not* his. She was mine. And I really hoped that she felt the same.

Gunnie walked up to my left and stared down at Hanlen. "Will she be okay?" she asked, and I let out a breath at hearing her voice.

"Physically? I think she'll be fine. Mentally . . . only time will tell."

"That's fair," she said and reached out before dropping her hand, realizing that she couldn't touch Hanlen. "I . . ." she started, and I looked at her. "I think she saw me before she passed out." She looked up at me then. "Is that possible?"

That surprised me. "I'm not sure. I *do* know she's sensitive, at the very least. Why do you say that?" I asked.

"She just looked right at where I was standing, and I saw her eyes widen before she sucked in a deep breath. And then she was out. Actually, I think she might have sensed me even earlier than that. I checked in on her at The Ravisan when she first got here and found a malevolent spirit taunting her. She probably thought she was dreaming when she woke to that nightmare, but she definitely knew we were there. That's actually when I infused a bit of my soul into the necklace."

"Interesting. Well, we can delve into that more when she wakes again. You did good." I looked up and spoke a little louder. "You all did good. So good.

Thank you all for being here. For helping. For being amazing."

Everybody nodded or said something in return, but before we could talk more, the place was flooded with police and EMTs and those of us not injured— or at least not severely—were ushered out to the lawn to answer a bunch of questions. When they finally wheeled Hanlen out on a gurney, I told Stephanie I'd finish my statement later and jogged to catch up to the paramedics. I didn't give them a chance to tell me that I couldn't ride with her since she wasn't family. I simply jumped into the back of the ambulance and dared them with a death glare to say anything.

The guy just shrugged and hopped in after me, and the woman got behind the wheel and headed off, lights and sirens blaring. While Hanlen was still unconscious, I held her hand gently and whispered encouraging words, surrounding her with healing energy and hoping for the best.

A FEW HOURS LATER, my arm bandaged and local anesthetic wearing off, I walked back into Hanlen's room, cup of terrible hospital coffee in hand. They'd stitched her up in the emergency room and gave her a transfusion, but because of her concussion and the amount of blood she'd lost, they wanted her to stay for a couple of days for observation. Hanlen's gorgeous, dark, silky hair was spread around her on the pillow, her face relaxed in rest. She looked like an angel, and I felt my heart skip a beat. I didn't want to disturb her, but I wanted to be closer. I moved to the far side of the bed and took a seat on the hard, blue vinyl chair, content to just watch her sleep for now.

As I sat back and the chair squeaked, Hanlen cracked her eyes open and turned her head in the direction of the sound. "Hey," she said, her voice scratchy and weak.

"Hey, yourself, gorgeous. How do you feel?"

"Like I was kidnapped by a sadistic serial killer who had totally lost touch with reality and then almost killed. Oh, wait, I was." She coughed, and I set down my coffee and moved to pour her a glass of water, bringing the straw to her lips.

"Just a few sips."

She did as I instructed and then lay back again against the pillow with a sigh. "What happened while I was out?" she asked.

"We got him, Hanlen. He's in police custody. I know the cops still need to talk to you, but we all gave our statements and there's no way he's getting off. I can't even imagine he'll get leniency for mental illness. He knew exactly what he was doing."

She stared off into space for a moment. "It's all just so surreal. I'm not sure I'll ever be able to process it."

"It's going to take time for all of us. I worked with

Remy for five years. While he was always a little different, I never in a million years would have guessed that he was so soulless, capable of taking another's life without regret. With fucking *pride*."

"He was really good at being who people expected him to be. And it didn't help that he really and truly believed in his so-called mission. I honestly thought I was going to die, and he tried to make me believe that it was an *honor*." I saw a tremble travel through her body.

I scooted the chair closer, grasped her hand again, and looked deep into her amber eyes, my heart swelling with gratitude that she was here with me. "I almost lost you," I said and brushed a piece of hair back from her forehead with my free hand.

"I thought I'd lost everything," she replied and looked at me. I felt as if she were looking into my soul, not just my eyes. "I didn't think I'd ever see you again."

"You're here. I'm here. Nobody's going anywhere. There is something I need to tell you, though."

"God, Dev. What is it with you and these we-need-to-talk conversations?" She smiled, and it lifted some of the weight from my shoulders.

I chuckled, but then sobered. "When the ghosts came to me and told me I needed to get to the cemetery, I had no idea why, but my instincts told me it was important. When I got there and found out that you were in that mausoleum and in danger, I wanted to rip apart the world, but I was stuck. I've never felt that way before, Hanlen. So frantic and terrified. And defeated. I love my family and my friends, even care about my clients. But I've never wanted to burn the earth to ensure that someone else was okay and safe. I'd realized it before, but in that moment, I knew, without a doubt, that I loved you."

She sucked in a breath but remained silent.

"I love you, Hanlen Arbor. I know this is really fast, but when you know, you know. The minute I ran into you on that sidewalk and looked into those amazing eyes, I knew that my soul was a match for yours. I know that some of yours is already spoken for. I understand that you will always love my cousin and she will always hold a huge piece of your heart, but I really hope that you can find some room for me, too. At least, eventually."

She still just stared at me, unblinking, not speaking, and I felt a tremble of apprehension trickle through me.

"I . . ." I started again and cleared my throat. "I don't expect you to say it. Hell, I'm not even sure how you really feel about me, and I probably just scared the shit out of you, but . . . if you'll have me, I want to be yours. Let me love you."

"Oh, Dev, I . . ." she started, and my heart dropped. Had I misread things so spectacularly? Was I only a source of fun while she was in town? No, I didn't think so.

"You don't have to say anything more," I said and sat back in my chair. "I know this is probably a lot." She immediately shifted in the bed and reached for me, wincing and grunting with the pain.

"Fucking hell," she said. "Holy shit, that hurts." I couldn't stand to see her in pain and stood, moving to her side again, her hand once more in mine.

"Let's try that again," she said and let out a little laugh. "What I was going to say is that I love you, too. It's insane and crazy and makes absolutely no sense, but it is what it is. I knew days ago, I just didn't know how you would take it, and I knew—I *know*—we have some hurdles to overcome, but you are the first person who has made me feel alive in a decade. You soothe my hurts. You make me laugh. You opened a whole new world to me, one I thought was utter nonsense until you showed me the beauty of it. You gave me life, and you gave me Ray. Through our combined memories, she will always live on."

I leaned in and kissed her. I was gentle; I didn't want to hurt her, but I needed to show her with actions as well as words how much she meant to me. When I pulled back, despite the somewhat chasteness of the kiss, we were both breathless. I had a feeling that chemistry, that utter rightness, would never change between us.

"Speaking of Ray," she said and looked into my eyes. "I think I saw her, Dev. I don't know, maybe I was hallucinating from the blood loss and shock, but right before I passed out in the crypt, I swore I saw her. She looked just like she did the night I lost her." Tears swam in her eyes for a moment.

I smiled. "She was there," I said. "And she mentioned that she thought that you may have seen her. How are you feeling about that?"

"How did I see her?" she asked.

"My guess?" I started. "It probably has something to do with getting hit on the head and the fact that you were in the middle of my and Lark's combined magic at the time. The day I met you, I knew you were sensitive. You reacted to things that most people don't and didn't even realize it. I knew then that it wouldn't take much to open your senses."

"Wow, okay," she said. "That's a bit to process. Not even two weeks ago, I didn't believe in any of this stuff and thought what you did was a bunch of bullshit."

I laughed. I couldn't help it. "Oh, I know," I said wryly.

"Now, I've been in the middle of it all and I can't dispute what I saw. But seeing ghosts . . . that's going to take some getting used to."

"I'll help you th—" Before I could even finish the sentence, a knock sounded on the door. Both Hanlen and I looked over and saw Detective Stephanie Miller standing in the doorway.

"Hey, guys," she said and walked in. "Sorry to bother you. How are you feeling, Hanlen?"

"I've been better," Hanlen answered. "But at least I'm alive."

"I just wanted to stop in and give you guys some updates." She leaned against the wall and looked at us. "Remy Dee Reaume will never be able to hurt anybody again. I would actually be surprised if he *doesn't* get the death penalty. Surprisingly, he confessed to fifteen murders. I think he's still proud of them and feels justified. Plus, he has your kidnapping and attempted murder. We had the forensic psychologist question him almost immediately and he said that Remy is one-hundred-percent sane and knew exactly what he was doing, so any bullshit insanity defense his lawyers may want to try will hopefully fail spectacularly."

"How does someone even end up that way?" Hanlen asked. "I mean, I know it happens, I've seen it, dealt with it in varying degrees in even my career, but he was scary."

"In Remy's case, I'm not sure there was any environmental reason. Some people are just born that way. From what we can dig up, he wasn't abused, he never had any injuries that could have contributed to his devolving morality. And what we uncovered at his house during our search leads us to believe that he's been this way from a very young age."

"Jesus Christ," Hanlen breathed.

"Yeah, it was messed up. I probably shouldn't be telling you this, but I know with everything you've been through and given your occupation, Hanlen, I feel like I can tell you. You know Remy lived way out in the bayou, right, Dev? Well, his home was a horror show. We found trophies from all of his victims in a loose floorboard in his home. He also had a stockpile of those creepy, hexagonal copper *memento mori* skull coins that he was using as his kill signature. But that's not even the worst part."

"Oh, I can't wait to hear this," I said, sarcasm dripping from my tone.

"He had an industrial-sized freezer in his garage," Stephanie continued. "Inside, we found the dismembered remains of his parents. We think they've been in there for at least ten years, if not longer. Nobody even knew that they were missing. Somehow, he found a way to make it look like they were loners. Perpetuated the charade that they were still alive and fine while utilizing their resources. This guy's sick. He's smart, manipulative, and I'm so sorry that it took you guys getting hurt for us to stop him, but I am beyond grateful that we did."

"Unbelievable," I breathed. "I still can't believe I didn't know. I can't believe nothing tipped me off. What good is having the power I have if I can't use it to uncover things like this and keep those I care about safe?"

"Dev," Stephanie said and moved forward to grip my hand. "Please don't beat yourself up over this. While this is a first in my career, I've spoken to enough federal profilers and talked to many cops and agents who work violent crimes. Most times, people don't know. I mean, look at history. For the most part, the most prolific serial killers were all brought low by happenstance. Nobody knew. They're really good at hiding who they are. Concealing the evil inside. Remy was liked by just about everybody who met him. This isn't on you."

I ran a hand over my hair and looked at Hanlen, brushing my fingers across her soft cheek as I took my seat in the chair once more.

"Well," Stephanie said and twisted her ponytail before letting it rest over her shoulder. "That's all I had. I just wanted to check in on you both and fill you in. Hanlen, we will need to get your official statement when you're ready, but it hasn't stopped us from moving forward."

"Of course," Hanlen said.

"I'll leave you two to it," the detective said and backed towards the door. "Call me if you need anything, but get better. Both of you." She waved and headed out the door, leaving Hanlen and me alone once again.

"So, what now?" Hanlen asked. I wasn't sure the breadth of her question, so I waited a beat to see if she'd elaborate. "I mean, for us. We don't even live in the same state."

"Well, in the short term, and despite everything, we need to finish this show." I quirked a smile. "We're still a day away from concluding the investigation. The good news is that it's not live and the delay shouldn't hurt anything with the network since we're shooting in advance for this episode, but we do need to finish. I'd really like for this to air in two weeks. Which means, I still need access to your property. Which further means, you're going to have to stick around for a little bit longer."

She flashed me that cheeky grin of hers that always made me feel lighter. "I think something can be arranged."

"After that . . ." I let the statement trail off and waited to see if she'd say more. When she didn't, I figured now was as good a time as any.

I blew out a breath. "So, I've been thinking. How settled are you in Texas?"

"My business is there," she answered, "but I do a lot of traveling already, can work virtually anywhere, and my one-bedroom apartment is nothing special. My lease is even up soon, and I haven't once thought about renewing. Why do you ask?"

My trepidation eased a bit. She seemed open to at least exploring options. I really hoped she'd like to think about what I was going to suggest at a mini-mum. "This might be impulsive, but I don't feel that way, and I hope you won't either. What do you think about moving back to New Orleans? You have a gorgeous house just sitting here, you have me, new friends, and if you're open to it, I can even give you some work while you settle in with Arbor Investigations here in Louisiana. I can always use additional investigators. And now that we lost Burke,"—I felt sadness well at the thought of the man whose life was cut way too short—"I could use some extra help."

She seemed to think about it for a minute, but she didn't immediately rebuff the idea, nor did she seem particularly opposed to it. "I love this city. I always have. I only moved because being here hurt too much. Now that you've opened my eyes to things that were previously well beyond my comprehension, and I know that, while no longer with me, Ray is fine, there's really no reason for me *not* to live here. You're right. Arborwood should be lived in. Enjoyed. It should be taken care of by those with a connection to the place and not trashed by vacationers. We've made enough money on the rental site that I could use it to take care of the property while enjoying it. It's mine by birthright, and Mom won't ever be coming back. There's really no reason not to use it now."

Hoped surged, but I could see that she was working through a few more things.

"Plus, I think it'd be good for Bea to have someone close who loves her."

"You are absolutely right," I said, feeling even more hopeful.

"And as for work, as I said, I can set up shop anywhere. I've already gotten offers on my office space since it's in such a coveted part of the city there.

I could easily use the money I make off that to buy something here. Or I could convert the carriage house into my office and work from Arborwood. It's not so far out of the city that clients couldn't find me."

She looked at me then, raising her eyes from our clasped hands, and I felt a massive surge of happiness pass through me. I knew what she would say, but I had to ask anyway. "So?"

She smiled, and the look she gave me made me feel complete. "Let's do it."

I kissed her then, being careful of her wounds but breathing in all that was Hanlen Arbor. "I love you."

"I love you, too, ghost man."

We both laughed.

Epilogue

Hanlen

I stood in the center of the open French doors, looking out into the courtyard at those gathered. Schuyler and Padre stood near the long table laden with snacks and food, talking with Bea and picking over a tray of appetizers we'd had catered. I wasn't sure what Padre and Sky's story was. They seemed close, but they also bickered constantly, and Schuyler was forever giving Paxton crap about his religion. He seemed to take it in stride but did occasionally tell her to mind her own damn business, though he was always nice about it.

We'd brought in some super comfortable outdoor furniture, and Van, Halen, and Dakota sat on one of the couches in front of the huge projection screen we'd set up for tonight, Dakota and Van play-fighting over Lennie's lap as she shoved at them both, laughing but telling them to get off her. I'd found out after our action-packed night here during night two of the shoot, the night I'd almost seen my life flash before my eyes, that Dakota and Van had been friends forever. It seemed the three were like siblings, and it made me smile.

Lark sat on one side of a small table, while Harper sat on the other side. Lark passed Harper her drink, and the psychologist took a sip, smiling over at the enigmatic witch. *Witch*. It was so weird that words like that, *Vodou*, *spells*, *psychic mediums*, *magic*, and *ghosts* were a normal part of my vocabulary now. My transformation from skeptic to believer had been a bit of a trial by fire, but I didn't regret it. Especially not with everything it had given me, even amidst August's and Burke's memorials as a reminder of what we'd also lost.

James and Aaron were around here somewhere, but I hadn't seen them in a bit. I had a feeling they might be out back, partaking in some herbaceous party favors. James had a bad back and mentioned that he always had a good medicinal stash. And after securing Remy in the mausoleum, he was kind of milking it by convincing Dev to let him partake on the job.

I took in the space again, noting the people in my

life now, my friends who felt more like family. And then I slewed my gaze over to the corner near the topiaries, taking in the other group gathered there.

A beautiful woman in a white, off-the-shoulder dress—Wren—embracing a handsome man with piercing dark eyes—Findley. A soldier in full historical garb, chatting with a good-looking guy who looked as if he should be a surfer if not for the wire-rimmed glasses. Burke smiled at something Desmond said, and it made my heart happy to see that death hadn't ruined everything. These people still had each other. They had us, though in a different capacity. They still had an existence they enjoyed.

Dev had been worried that his sister and her guy may leave now that the identity of her murderer had been uncovered, but they'd told him in no uncertain terms that he wasn't getting rid of them that easily. They enjoyed being his investigators, just as Desmond loved being Dev's runner, jettisoning all over to talk to other ghosts and relay information. And Burke was grateful that he could continue his research for the show. I could see it. It gave them purpose. Made them feel connected. And the fact that they were free labor didn't hurt.

My gaze moved to the other side of Wren, to the woman who stopped talking to Findley and looked my way. I smiled and waved. I would give just about anything to give Ray a huge hug, but just having her in my life again was a gift I never expected to receive.

The fact that I could now see ghosts was still really freaking strange, but it also made me ridiculously happy. Dev had even worked a spell on my necklace that let me hear them if they wanted me to. Ray and I had had a really long conversation, and I'd gotten to say all the things to her that I hadn't gotten to say before Remy ripped us apart. There was closure in that, and now was a new chapter.

I looked across the gathered crowd of both living and dearly departed and gave myself a little internal shake. This was my life now. How strange and utterly wonderful. I felt strong arms wrap around me from behind and smelled Dev's amazing oak moss scent before he leaned down and breathed in my ear. "Penny for your thoughts," he said and kissed my neck, making goose bumps erupt on my skin.

"I was just taking in our strange family out there and thinking how great it is."

"It is pretty great, isn't it?" he agreed. "So, are you ready to see yourself on TV?"

I groaned. "I don't know. But I am curious to see how it all came together."

"I can't wait for everybody to see it. I may be biased, but this is one of my favorite finished products. It's so good, Hanlen. And the evidence is super compelling. The network thinks that this episode may open the way for more viewership. It's very . . . personal, and it shows in how it all came together."

He turned me and kissed me, and I melted into him. "Thank you for that. For everything."

"I should be thanking you," I said. "You rid me of my ghosts, as ironic as that statement is."

He laughed. "And you, mine—except for those we want to keep around," he added and looked over at our laughing group of dearly departed.

"You know," he added, "those in my religion have a belief. Well, we have many,"—he chuckled—"but this one is important for this moment. We believe that the soul and spirit are initially split. We believe that upon death, the *gros-bon-ange*, or good big angel, stays with the body for some time and eventually becomes part of the lwa—those unique and powerful spirits we serve. On the other hand, the *ti-bon-ange*, the good little angel, functions as a guardian and protector. When and if revived through ritual, the *gros-bon-ange* can become a *govi*, inhabiting an earthly vessel to remain with those they love and to be called upon by people like me. We are lucky enough to have those, you and I. Spirits who love us enough to remain."

I swiped a tear from my cheek and nodded. "And now I can see and interact with them. A gift that you gave me."

He kissed me. "You're the gift, Hanlen."

This man. My phone suddenly rang with a familiar tune.

"That's probably my mom on video chat," I said

and stepped back just enough to pull my cell from my pocket to answer the call.

"Hey, Mom," I said and took in my mother on the screen. Linette Arbor-Dunhill was a beautiful woman who fit in well with the elite, spandex-wearing, Botox-chasing, yoga-retreat-attending ladies of Boca Raton.

"Hi, sweetie. Hi, handsome," she said to Dev. Mom had been all too thrilled when I called to tell her that Dev and I were together and that I was moving back to Arborwood. She even told me that her psychic had told her that would happen and that she kind of already knew. The old me would have scoffed at her and told her that she should adjust her meds. The new me could only smile. Because . . . who knew? Maybe her psychic was like Larken. Lark could be so intuitive it was kind of scary at times.

"Hi, Mrs. Dunhill."

"I told you, call me Linette," my mom corrected.

"Are you ready for the premiere?" I asked, and my mom nodded enthusiastically. "I so am. I cannot wait to see the old homestead and you guys on television. I'm so happy that you had such a wonderful trip initially and that you decided to return for the airing." We hadn't told her what'd happened with Remy a couple of weeks ago. At least, not yet. It had been tough to avoid chatting with her on video as I healed, but I still felt it was the right decision. She would likely find out eventually, but we didn't want to worry her right now. Everything was taken care of, and nobody was in danger any longer. I figured I could tell her when I was settled back here in New Orleans for good. Especially since I pretty much knew that once she heard and found out we knew who'd killed Reagan, she'd want to hop on a plane immediately and make sure I was okay. See for herself, in person, that I was all right. And, surprisingly, I was okay with that.

She turned to her left and accepted a glass of wine from someone just off screen. "Thanks, hon," she said and blew a kiss before looking back at the screen. "Your stepfather says hello."

"Tell him hi from us. Are you guys watching alone?"

"No," she said. "We have two sets of neighbors over. They're in the other room getting drinks and filling up on appetizers. What about you guys? Romantic night?"

"Not at all, actually. But, even better. Here, hold on." I flipped the view of the screen and panned the camera across the courtyard at the assembled guests. I wished that Mom could see Ray, but it was enough for me to know that she could see my mom. I looked over and saw her nodding with a sad smile. I waved from behind the camera where my mom couldn't see.

"Hey, guys," I called. Everybody turned to look at me. "Say hi to my mom, Linette. The previous owner of Arborwood. Mom, as I'm sure you'll recognize, this is the cast and crew of *Haunted New Orleans*."

"Oh my gosh," I heard my mom say, and Dev smiled at me. "Brilliant stars. All of you. I absolutely love you all. Thank you for taking on Arborwood and getting us some answers."

I flipped the camera back around and got both Dev and me in the frame. "Thanks for calling, Mom." Just as I said that, someone extinguished the lights in the courtyard, the only illumination coming from the citronella tiki torches we had set up around the place, and the sound came on, the network's logo showing on the massive screen.

"I think that's our cue," I said and smiled at my mother. "Enjoy the show. Call me tomorrow?" I asked. "I'm not headed back to Texas to pack up and get things squared away there for another day or two."

"Of course, sweetie. Oh my gosh, I'm so excited," she said and bounced in her seat. It made me smile. She placed her fingers against her lips. "*Mwah, mwah, mwah.*" She blew us kisses. "Go. Enjoy. Love you."

"I love you, too, Mom."

"You, too, Deveraux," she added.

"The feeling's mutual, Linette."

Mom winked and disconnected, and I cuddled into Dev again, his strong arms coming around me.

"What do you say, gorgeous?" he said. "Ready to join everybody and check out this show? I hear it's pretty good."

"Yeah, I suppose that'd be okay," I teased. "On one condition."

"What's that?" he asked.

"That as soon as the credits roll, we kick everybody out, and you take me to bed immediately."

He turned us, slung an arm around my shoulders, and kissed my temple. "I think that can be arranged."

Just as we started walking, the atmospheric theme music for *Haunted New Orleans* filled the space, and Dev's gorgeous face and melted-chocolate voice came on screen, followed by shots of each of the others in action. Schuyler handed me a glass of whiskey with ginger ale, and when I heard, *"This . . . is Haunted New Orleans,"* I knew that those five words would always mean more to me now. The truth had set me free.

I was finally home.

THE END

Haunted New Orleans Series

Coming in 2022 is Malum Discordiae, the second book in the Haunted New Orleans Series

When knowledge and temptation collide, the fall only needs a forbidden fruit.

For more information, click here:
https://www.ladybosspress.com/rayvnsalvador

Acknowledgments

To my friends and family who support me in every-thing I do . . . and it's a lot at times, thank you from the bottom of my heart!

An extra-special thanks to my badass publishing team. You guys are rock stars!

Always, *always* to my wonderful editor, Laura, who never fails to make me feel good about my craft, and my steadfast betas—Erika, Brandon, Michelle, and Katrina . . . thank you! I love you guys tons. I also wouldn't feel nearly as good about this without thoughts from Marissa, who served as my younger generation gauge, so she deserves a major shoutout here, too. I appreciate you, girl!

I'd also like to send a huge thank you and much love to my forever partner in crime, Jen Vayda, who shoved down her fear and joined me for a whirlwind of a trip over Halloween and the Day of the Dead in

New Orleans several years back. And the premiere Voodoo Mambo of New Orleans, Bloody Mary, who took us on a rollercoaster of a ride, dipping into tantalizing niches of New Orleans, showing us and teaching us so very much. Things that only the most fortunate—or those who live it—get to see. We experienced more in seven days than I think most do in a lifetime. I will carry those memories forever, and the things that happened on our insane and once-in-a-lifetime trip were the beautiful fuel for the fire that is now the Haunted New Orleans series.

And last—but most certainly not least—you, dear readers. Thank you for taking a chance on me. For leaving encouraging reviews and sharing about my books far and wide. For sending me notes of wonder and praise. By reading the words between these pages, you are literally making my dreams come true. You are the absolute best!

Also available from Rayvn
Salvador

The Willow Falls series:

Your Move

Seasons Change

The Fourth and Goal Series:

Blue Forty-Two

Blind Side

The Haunted New Orleans Series:

Eternal Spark – a Haunted New Orleans short story
freebie

Memento Mori

Coming soon…

Malum Discordiae

Mea Culpa

About Rayvn Salvador

Rayvn Salvador is a lifelong bibliophile who left her eighteen-year IT career in Software Quality Assurance to live her dream: getting paid to read as a full-time editor (done as her alter ego), and to write when the mood strikes. She lives in Florida with three crazy cats and her incredibly supportive beau, dreaming about the Midwest's changing leaves as she perfects her yoga poses on the beach.

Website: http://rayvnsalvador.com

 facebook.com/RayvnSalvador

 twitter.com/RayvnSalvador

 instagram.com/rayvnsalvador

 bookbub.com/profile/rayvn-salvador

Praise for Rayvn Salvador

"Rayvn Salvador pens an exhilarating and romantic tale you don't want to miss!"

~USA Today Bestselling Author Jen Talty

"An exciting new author!"

~USA Today Bestselling Author Michele Hauf

"Rayvn is a great storyteller!"

~5-Star Amazon reviewer

"Words that bring vivid imagery, along with swoon-worthy feels."

~USA Today Bestselling Author Tigris Eden/J.K Rivers

CPSIA information can be obtained
at www.ICGtesting.com
Printed in the USA
BVHW032101171021
619165BV00005B/41

9 781648 181184